Rasa Aškinytė

Rasa Aškinytė is one of a new generation of celebrated Lithuanian novelists recreating what Lithuanian fiction looks like. She has a Master's degree in philosophy and teaches at the Lithuanian University of Educational Sciences. She has written four novels and an introduction to philosophy for children and was awarded the Lithuanian Book of the Year in 2014.

About the translator

Jura Avizienis teaches writing at Boston University. She has been translating Lithuanian literature since 1990 when her first translations appeared in Violeta Kelertas's anthology of contemporary Lithuanian fiction, Come Into My Time (University of Illinois Press). Since then her translations have appeared in The Vilnius Review, The Dedalus Book of Lithuanian Literature and Best European Fiction. She has translated two of Rasa Aškinytė's novels: The Easiest and The Man Who Needed Nothing.

Rasa Aškinytė

The Easiest

Translated from Lithuanian
by Jūra Avizienis

Noir

First published in Lithuanian as Lengviausias

Published by Noir Press.
www.noirpress.co.uk
noirpress@hotmail.com

Cover design by Le Dinh Han
Model: Phoebe Jolly

978-0-9955600-1-7

This story is based on real events. Any resemblance between this story and your life, dear reader, are purely intentional.

I

THE BOOK OF TIME

*'Thou shalt not make unto thee any graven image, or
any likeness of anything that is in heaven above, or that
is in the earth beneath, or that is in the water under the
earth. Thou shalt not bow down thyself to them, nor serve
them· for I the Lord thy God am a jealous God, visiting
the iniquity of the fathers upon the children unto the
third and fourth generation of them that hate me.'*

(God's Second Commandment from the Book of Exodus)

Here We Go Again . . .

or

Usually things are simpler than they appear to be.

MY NAME is Tom. No, my name is Blanca*. My name is Blanca. I'm 35, although I was 30 not too long ago. Years don't always follow in chronological order. Is there anything you can do about that? Can you make time obey you? Of course you can't. Nobody can. Nobody even bothers to give it an honest try. So we travel together; time on its course, and I on mine.

I have a sister. And that's something. Not everyone has a sister. I'd like a brother too, but I don't have one. My sister is so much older than I, that sometimes I think of her as my mother. Once I asked her if she was. She didn't say a word, but my mother said, "You're mad." That's how she answers every other question I ask, so I try to ask fewer questions.

Sometimes the way I talk is odd, and I even look odd. My sister says it's nothing; sooner or later this happens to everyone. She's right. But my mother never says, "You're mad!" to her. And my mother's right. Everyone's always right, except me. And that's fine.

---

* Name has been changed

Oh, and another thing I forgot to mention; I don't actually exist.

Every now and then I live with a guy. If you were to ask if he was my husband, I wouldn't know what to say. He's a guy. It's as simple as that. When I'm not living with someone, I live alone. I have my own apartment – to be more precise, it's a few rooms on the first floor of an old wooden cottage. There's no second floor. There's a ground floor that's occupied. Sometimes someone sleeps in the stairwell. It's someone different every night – or maybe they just change their clothes. But the reek is always the same. I've never understood if it was a man or a woman. Sometimes they wear a skirt, but that doesn't mean anything. The 'someone' never sleeps in anyone's way. They always make their bed in the corner, but still they manage to annoy everyone. I don't know why. Maybe that's the kind of person they are.

They bother me too. Another thing that bothers me is that there are no stairs to the first floor. So, how do I get to my apartment, you might well ask. Maybe there's a lift? Oh, come on! Where would they put a lift in a house like that? And what would hold it up? Well, it might be very light I suppose. Anyway, nobody lives on the first floor. Only me. Have you ever seen a lift made just for one person? I have.

I use a ladder. It's difficult if I've bought too much; I have to make several trips. But it's no big deal, the ladder's lovely, I painted it myself. And my apartment's lovely too, but if I'm living with someone, it's usually at his place, because it's one thing to get someone to live with you, but quite another to get them to climb up a ladder.

I realise I'm only describing my better qualities, but this is no "SWF seeks . . ." ad, so there's no reason to lie.

I don't have any children. Which is a pity.

I work at *France*. That's the name of the café where I wash dishes. Just don't think that's what I do for a living. No, my actual job is counting the money. I wash dishes because I want to (I like to watch how the dirty water runs down the drain). That's one of the jobs they don't pay me for. They pay me for all the other jobs I do, and they pay me well.

For example, sometimes I play music for money because I know how to play the French horn. Not many people do. I was already working at *France* when I started playing. I didn't choose the instrument by chance; I liked the fact that the sound has to flow through four metres of coiled brass tubing. And I liked the teacher. I lived with him for a few months. I don't remember how many.

I saw him for the first time at *France*.

I think where you see someone for the first time is important. First impressions are made quickly, and not just on our clothing, but also where we meet. For example, there's a huge difference between meeting someone at the airport or in the archives, at the library or at an Off-License, in Nuremburg or at a nursery, on St. Kit or in a kitchen. Dakar or a dog show. Hyde Park or in a harem, etc., etc.

Pathological microorganisms
or
Usually what is harmless on the outside leads to disease when ingested.

PATHOLOGICAL MICROORGANISM − a disease-causing microorganism. A pathological microorganism enters the body, destroys a portion of its cells and tissues, or harms it otherwise, thus causing disease. The most common pathological microorganisms are viruses, bacteria, and fungi. Also included among these are protists, for example, malaria-causing protozoa.

So, the first time I saw him was at *France*.

He was at the bar. This didn't seem at all unusual; all lonely, single men hang out at the bar. That's why I didn't notice that his legs were too short. Not bowlegged, just too short. Both of them equally.

He immediately asked me to marry him. I said no because I was a minor, and I didn't feel like asking for my mother's permission. He said I didn't look like a minor. I told him things are not always as they appear.

Although the bar was dark, it was plain to see that he was attractive. He had a strange expression on his face, as if he were prepared for something, but it was hard to tell what. It looked like he was about to start laughing, or crying. But he didn't. (Not then, not later.)

He was performing that night, which was odd, because nobody plays the French horn in bars. Two girls were performing with him, but I'm not sure what their instruments were called. They played well. Their trio was called "Twilight's Darkness." I have never heard a more insipid name. People feel compelled to name everything. Especially one another. Have you ever known anyone without a name? I'm sure you haven't. I'm also sure that not many people have actually earned their name, even the shortest.

They were playing well, but I couldn't enjoy the music because one of the girls from the trio was annoying me; just when you find something to enjoy, something starts to annoy you. The two things are inextricably linked.

For the entire time the girl played she faced the man on the French horn, not the audience. This wasn't very comfortable because the French horn player was right at the back of the stage, so she turned to face him there. The girl wasn't pretty – she really was 'twilight'. She had long arms, long black hair, colourless eyes. I don't like people with colourless eyes.

And the man watched the girl the whole time he played. I didn't like that. If they wanted to stare at each other, they could do that at home. There was no reason for them to come to my bar.

I've always wanted what others have. There's nothing I can do about this. I'm not responsible for the diseases I'm afflicted with.

The man probably didn't like the girl's colourless eyes either, he attempted to look down. He was watching her as if he wished to pierce her skin and enter her. I wanted to tell him that you can't look at people like that. When you try to penetrate someone, you create the desire to resist.

I waited for the concert to end. I wanted to tell the man that I too knew how to play. I played the Piano. I think playing piano has an effect on you; doing one thing with one hand and something else with the other causes your brain to develop differently. You become different from everyone else: you become an artist. I was an artist, and I wanted everyone to know it.

As it became clear later, the French horn player had one failing: he couldn't, or, perhaps, wouldn't pronounce my name properly. He'd say, "Blianca, I love you so much." My name is ugly as it is, but when you pronounce it like that it becomes unbearable. This "Blianca" was the reason why, one morning, I moved back to my place, leaving him with all my stuff.

Whenever I moved in with a man, I would take as few things with me as possible. Because of the ladder. Perhaps I chose an apartment like this intentionally, because it's not things that matter, but the soul. In effect, I was caring for my soul.

At France there are as many tables as you want

or

Usually people only ask the obvious.

THERE ISN'T a table in my apartment. I don't know whose fault that is. I could best use a table in the big room, but the floor in there tilts so much that even if I had one, everything would slide off it. In the other room, the floor is as level as can be, like in the movies. You could put tables in all four corners if you wanted, but I'm not going to. If I can't put something where I want it, then I don't need it at all.

At *France* there are as many tables as you could ever desire. That's why I like it there better than at home.

"Twilight's Darkness" had stopped playing. One of the women left right after the show, and the other, the one with colourless eyes, just sat and stared. Only at the television now, not at the man.

"Congratulations to the winners. Until tomorrow," said the pretty woman on the screen.

People like to win. I don't know if I've ever won anything. Obviously I have my apartment, my job at *France*, and a couple of other things. If I said that to my mother, she would say, "You're mad. That's not winning." But if you're happy about something, then you have won.

I didn't understand why the woman with colourless eyes didn't go home. She sat there even though she no longer had anything to wait for; I'd already won over her French horn player. He had been sitting at the bar for more than an hour staring at me. I can't remember his name. I think it was Blanca. No, that can't be right.

I asked him if he wanted to be a star.

"What do you mean?" the French horn player asked.

"If you were famous like Einstein, they'd write about you in encyclopedias and sell your action figure at McDonald's along with wind-up monkeys and transformers," I explained.

"I see," said the French horn player.

I couldn't be bothered to ask again, even though I still didn't understand if he wanted to be famous or not.

"I can teach you to play," the French horn player suggested.

We both understood what he meant by that, so I didn't say anything.

"Do you know why there aren't any elephants in Antarctica?" I asked, to change the subject.

"Of course," said the French horn player. "They're too heavy; they can't take a single step without breaking through the ice. And nobody can survive if they can't move a single step."

I liked the fact that he knew everything. That was my main reason for moving in with him the following week. You find that odd? What's so odd about it? Everyone does it. How can something that everyone does be odd?

"Do you like colourless eyes?" I asked, loud enough for everyone in the bar to hear.

"No," the French horn player replied. I don't know if he understood why I had raised my voice, but he shouted back.

"What kind of eyes do you like?" I asked, a little more quietly.

"Closed eyes," the French horn player answered. Or maybe he said something else. Maybe I just wanted him to answer that way.

It was winter

or

Usually you can only prove what's already obvious. What's not obvious is practically impossible to prove.

IT WAS winter. It was clear that it was winter even though it was warm and it wasn't snowing. Some things are so obvious they don't need proving.

I strolled down the street with the French horn player; I was carrying a little bag, he was lugging his French horn. We walked arm in arm like real lovers. I had the impression that the woman with colourless eyes was tailing us. I wanted to make a snowball and throw it at her, but there wasn't any snow.

I understood, then, how skiers feel when they drive out to the mountains and there's no snow. You might say that snow is too unstable a substance for there to be enough of it just when you need it. But instability is no excuse. If all stable things just appeared and disappeared the world would be too unpredictable. Nobody could live in a world like that.

I wanted it to snow so that the French horn player would brush the snow from my face. Or so that I could brush it from his. That would have been perfect. After all, you can't touch someone's face without a reason the first time you meet.

But it wasn't snowing. It wasn't even raining. So we walked and talked. We walked in totally the opposite direction to my house. When I told him about my house he wouldn't believe it. Even I find it hard to believe that someone could live in such a house. But sometimes I convince myself. I'm just not sure how to convince others.

"Have you wanted to play the French horn since you were little?" I asked.

"No kid wants to be a French horn player, because no kid could imagine that you could be one."

"Well, I always dreamed of being a window-cleaner. I think pellucidity is the most beautiful quality of all," I said.

I couldn't relax. I was sure the woman, not realising she was already in his past, was still following us, trying to ruin our present and our future. I kept turning back and, although I couldn't see her, I needed no evidence to know she was there.

Even when we weren't walking arm-in-arm, the French horn player kept touching my hand as if by accident. I liked that. Though it was cold, I wasn't wearing gloves. I think it's important to let people touch you. Especially when nothing is yet clear, when everything is still up in the air.

"Do you believe that music can save the world?" I asked.

"I do," laughed the French horn player. "Everyone believes that. People were playing music before they started to speak."

"That's true. You can't solve anything by talking," I agreed. "People ruin everything by talking."

"Usually people think one thing and say something completely different. But music and dance don't lie."

"I never thought about it that way." I was surprised.

"Good."

"That's why people are afraid to sing and dance," I said, after some time. The French horn player had linked arms with me again. "You ask them to sing, but they say they don't know how. The same with dancing."

"I've never heard of anyone admitting that they don't know how to talk or that they have nothing to say."

Exactly. I usually don't have anything to say, but I talk endlessly. I have a talk prepared for every possible situation. Just ask me something and you won't be able to shut me up. You'll find out everything: where I've been, what I want, when I moved here, what hurts, or how I got hurt last year, what I bought, what I read, who I love, what I eat. I might also throw in a few childhood reminiscences, describe what plans I have. What a bore. Who could possibly care? I was smoking my fifteenth cigarette, even though every morning I vowed to smoke only three. I wasn't that far from my limit.

"When I smoke, I breathe at least a part of what I want to say into my lungs."

"Is that why smoking is bad for your health?" The French horn player laughed.

He had a nice laugh. I like people who have a nice laugh.

"Did you know that cows can climb up stairs as high as they want, but they can't climb

down?"

"That's very ambitious of them!" Now I was laughing.

"They don't have a choice."

"That's what they all say – I don't have a choice."

"Cows don't say that."

"Did anyone ask them?"

"If you don't ask, you'll never know."

"You know, there's a certain kind of person," I said, "who wants to give everything away."

"What do you mean, everything?"

"Everything they have."

"Are you that kind of person?" asked the French horn player.

"Yes."

"Then give me your clothes. It would be nice if you undressed right now," he was laughing again.

His laugh was so sincere. It was the best possible proof.

Stones don't bleed

or

Usually, having won something, you find that you never needed it in the first place.

I DON'T know who created the world, but I don't think it's very well designed. It would be much better if:

- Everyone agreed on all questions.
- There were fewer things in the world that one might desire.
- People didn't want what others had.

People waste most of their time on negotiations and distribution. If one person has no need for something, then nobody else needs it either. You don't believe me? I can prove it: landfills are full of things. But if one person were to suddenly need one of those things, then everyone would need it.

For example, I needed the French horn player. Why did the woman with colourless eyes suddenly need him too? One would think there were no other men in the world. Or no other couples to tail.

"Doesn't it seem like someone's following us?" I asked the French horn player.

He didn't even look back.

"Yes, our past is gaining on us," he said, almost too happily.

I don't know what annoyed me more, his groundless good humour, his refusal to cater to my whims, or that we had got to the bus stop and halted. I didn't want everything to end there.

"Where are you headed?" I asked mournfully. Unfortunately I'm no good at hiding my emotions.

"Let's sit for a while," the French horn player offered. He seemed tired of carrying that horn of his around.

We sat down, I on some kind of tar, though I didn't know it then, I would end up throwing those trousers away. It struck me then that the real consequences of our actions only become evident much later. But that night, not suspecting anything, I sat on the bench at the bus stop and was perfectly happy.

"When we're young, we know how to live well. Later on, we even learn how to be happy. We find out what pleasure is," said the French horn player.

I didn't understand what stage he was at. Not appreciating banalities, I asked him to play something for me.

"I could, but not at the bus stop. I don't play at bus stops," he said.

We both understood what that meant, so I didn't answer. For what seemed an eternity we sat quietly. Dogs barked*.

---

* There isn't a single novel that does not contain the sentence "Dogs were barking." Even in the Bible dogs are mentioned 14 times.

I've never understood why they bark so much. There are many things I don't understand, so eventually I stop thinking about them.

Although it was night and the buses had stopped running two hours before, more people gathered at the bus stop. Perhaps they too wanted to sit for a while. Nobody said or did anything, but it was clear that it was time for us to move. You can tell when you're being kicked out.

I had barely stood up when I stumbled on something, probably some kind of rock. Nothing terrible happened, because, after all, rocks don't bleed. At least nobody has ever proven the contrary. Though I have blood, I didn't bleed. I didn't fall, but twisted my ankle in such a way I could barely walk. I'm really sorry. I know this wasn't appropriate behaviour for a first date. I didn't do it on purpose. And besides, I was not to blame; the woman with colourless eyes was. There's no excuse for following people around and frightening them. You have to be able to admit defeat and come to terms with it. It's no good getting caught up in in the present's vicious circles; you need to look to the future.

I knew perfectly well how to do that.

I've always managed to get out of a situation before it started to deteriorate. Why wait until someone says, "I don't love you anymore. It's over." It's better to back out when everything is still wonderful, just as the first signs of restlessness are beginning to show. But you have to watch carefully. For example, if someone writes to me every day, and one day he writes in the afternoon, not in the morning, as usual, then I run. I don't say anything, I simply disappear. I never ask to be loved.

If someone can't meet me when I want them to, or if they don't arrive when I'm expecting them, then, so long! I don't need someone like that. But I also have no need for someone who caters to my every whim. I don't understand why they cling to me, why they don't leave me alone. I run from them too.

Just don't say I don't know what I want, because I do. I want to be in control of the situation. And that usually works for me.

Times like these
or,
Usually it's a pity to lose something.

AT SUCH times, it's hard to know whether you should grieve or celebrate, so I didn't do either.

The French horn player was a good man and he took me home. He asked the taxi to wait and helped me out, and making it clear he had no intention of kissing me, politely said goodbye and got back in the taxi. He didn't even ask how I was going to hobble up to my apartment. If he had asked, I would have told him it was none of his business.

During all the excitement, I lost my bag. It was a pity, but actually, I couldn't even remember what I had in it.

I'm not sure when the woman with colourless eyes disappeared. Perhaps she ran away when I hurt my ankle; her type always runs away as soon as there's a problem. Or perhaps she couldn't keep up with us after we got into the cab; she was fit, but I doubt she could run that fast. Or perhaps she managed to squeeze into the cab. After all, I didn't check the front seat. In that case she drove off with the French horn player.

It was too bad that I didn't have his phone number; I could have called him and asked. The question is whether he would have told the truth; in cases like that people usually lie.

I lie too. For example, I lie about not having any money. People take me for a fool who can't make a living. I'm quite happy for people to think I'm a fool. Then, at least for a while, they have to think about it, trying to decide if I've always been stupid, or whether it's the consequence of some extenuating circumstances. I'm not sure what conclusions they come to, because they always say the same thing: what a pity. I feel their response is a pity too. They feel sorry for me and I for them. Pity doesn't bring us together though; in fact, on the contrary, it alienates us totally. No matter how sorry I am, I'm not in the slightest bit sorry to lose them. I have no idea if they're sorry to lose me.

2084

or,

Usually what begins well ends badly. And vice versa.

380 BC was a leap year, beginning on a Wednesday according to the Gregorian calendar.

2084 will be a leap year, beginning on a Saturday according to the Gregorian calendar.

I DON'T like people who think they know what will happen in the future. I don't even know what happened in the past.

My mother always knows when nothing good will come of things. I don't know how she knows this; she's never met any of my boyfriends, but as soon as she catches a whiff that I have a new one she tries to convince me that, as usual, I shouldn't bother tormenting myself.

She never asks if he's blond, or dark haired, whether he's attractive or not, whereas to me that seems vital. After all, you can tell someone's future based on their appearance.

It's harder to tell his future if he doesn't ask for your phone number when he's saying goodnight. In these cases, even my mother suggests that I wait and see how things turn out. I don't really understand what 'wait and see' means. I can't wait because I have to go to work almost every day.

The following day, my ankle didn't hurt in the least; when you have to go to work, everything stops hurting.

The day was typical in other ways as well. People came and went; they ate.

The French horn player didn't show up that day or the next. When he finally did show up, he gave me a glass bead necklace as a gift. It was horrible. Just tell people what you like and they'll give it to you. They really have no imagination. To make matters worse, not only were the beads transparent, they were also uneven. The French horn player bragged that he'd made them himself. I have no idea how and where one makes a glass bead necklace and besides, I really don't like crafts. I think everything should be even and symmetrical.

I can't even stand handwriting. The letters are always so uneven and crooked that it's horrible to read, even when the words are pleasant. I agree completely with the popes who ordered heretical books burned, or the Emperors Ceasar, Aurelius, Theodosius I or the Arab king, Amr Ibn al'Aas, who stubbornly burned down the library of Alexandria. It makes no difference that the books were masterpieces. The fact that they were hand written ruined everything. They deserved to be burned, because they were ugly. I type everything; I love the evenly spaced letters. It makes what you want to say so much clearer.

I looked around the bar, but the woman with colourless eyes was nowhere to be seen. That was a good sign. After all, you can tell the future on such omens as well. For example, if someone says, "I can't live without you," that's a bad sign.

Just don't imagine that's what the French horn player said. He didn't. He did ask me why we hadn't seen each other for so long. That was a good question, but I didn't know how to answer, so I suggested that we stopped dwelling on the past.

The French horn player was almost always silent. I think silence is a good sign. If you want to predict the future, you can make inferences based on silence. It's a shame, then, that I don't know how to be quiet. Noise gives me a sense of security.

The French horn player liked to do nothing. When I didn't have to go to work, we would lie around in bed for hours without moving or talking. I liked lying around like that. Now I think that those hours were some of the best of my life. But I can't lie around like that for too long; it's important to move. But if anyone were to ask why, what's so great about constant movement and change? I wouldn't know how to answer them.

It's best to go to the cinema
or,
Usually people want you to get to know them, or at least to pretend that you do.

WHEN YOU don't know what to do, go to the cinema. Choose a film both of you will hate, because then, when you leave the theatre, you'll feel a stronger bond than ever before.

"I think films should be clear, simple, and beautiful – just like life," I said to the French horn player.

He didn't respond.

"I hate films that aren't realistic and are full of nonsense. For example, when, in the middle of a film, statues turn their heads and face the audience. All we need is for that to actually happen in real life!"

The French horn player ate, saying nothing. But I was sure he was listening.

I could never talk long because *France* was always full. A beautiful black girl came in every evening; her name was Polina. I rarely remember people's names, but hers I remembered. I doubt that meant anything.

Polina's blue hair* complemented her black eyes beautifully. Her beautiful shoulders were bare; she walked

---

* I assume it was dyed

gracefully. Only black women could be that beautiful; I could not take my eyes off her. The first night she came in I apologized to her; I told her I wouldn't be able to avoid looking at her. I told her that if she didn't like it, she would have to stop coming to *France,* because I couldn't stop going there, nor could I stop looking at her. It wasn't my fault she was so beautiful.

"Look all you want," Polina said.

That was a lovely thing to say, wasn't it? She wasn't pretentious in the least; we became best friends.

Polina was Polish. I never actually asked her if she was, I just assumed it from her name. After all, a name tells a lot about a person.

I gave Polina the glass bead necklace. Because they were no longer colourless, the beads looked beautiful around her neck. It was really lovely to see the right thing in the right place at the right time. The French horn player grimaced seeing them around her neck and didn't show up at *France* for two days; but time passes quickly and those days passed quickly too. Polina came in every night and we talked and laughed.

We decided to pretend not to know each other every other day. On those evenings, we would do as we pleased; talk to other people, eat, Polina would dance, and I would work as much as was needed. We would never get too close to each other because strangers don't behave like that. We wouldn't talk or even look at each other (I looked at her though). Those evenings, when we were strangers, were my favourite times.

*   *   *

I like to pretend I don't know the person I'm with. For some reason, though, most people don't particularly like this game. When I was little, I would pretend I didn't know my mother; in the middle of a shop, I would blurt out:

"Excuse me, missus, who are you?"

People would start looking at us suspiciously. My mother would flush with anger. This made her look very beautiful. She would grab me by the arm and try to drag me off somewhere to the side so she could give me a thrashing. I wouldn't give up. I'd kick and scream.

"What do you want from me, missus?"

"Little girl, do you know this lady?" someone would ask.

"No . . .' I'd stammer through my tears. 'I've never seen her in my life."

"Let go of the girl, M'am." The voices of the passersby would grow angrier, and my mother's face, redder.

"Let's go, Blanca. Be a good girl," My mother would plead.

"My name isn't Blanca!" I would scream. At this point I would pretend that I didn't even know who I was.

Sometimes we would tussle for a bit longer, sometimes less so, but in the end, someone would call the police and take us to the police station. Then I'd rush into my mother's arms crying.

"Mummy, mummy, where were you?"

Confused, the police would discharge us and send us home.

My mother would never get angry and leave me. Mothers like mine never abandon their children. It was different with my sister. One time I pretended not to know her as well.

"Thank God," my sister said and turned and left. I sat in the store manager's office for half a day until my mother came to get me.

My mother got to the point where she couldn't take me anywhere, until one day someone suggested she carry IDs for both of us.

Later I tried this game with men I was with, but they were never as easy as my mother. One time I was in a restaurant with one of my first boyfriends; after we'd eaten half of our dessert, I looked him in the eyes and said, "Who are you?"

He thought I was joking. He tried to say something, but I wouldn't give in.

"I've never met you before. What do you want from me? Why are you sitting at my table?"

Ignoring his answers, I asked the same questions again and again. After five minutes, he got annoyed. He paid the bill and tried to take me by the arm to escort me out.

"Don't touch me. I don't know you," I yelled across the restaurant. "I haven't finished my torte. What do you want from me? I don't even know you."

Finally the man left me there (I calmly finished eating and even ordered another drink). I never saw him again. Sometime later I heard that he was telling the story to everyone, declaring that he had no intention of ever seeing that crazy woman again.

Why does everyone mistake games for madness? To this day I don't understand what's so bad about the game. In the end it's not a game; we can never really know each other, so why pretend?

Not everyone is attractive,
or,
Usually it's hard to find a place where nobody has ever eaten.

POLINA AND I usually met at *France*, but sometimes she'd invite me to her place. Polina's apartment was also on the first floor, but in a new building. All her furniture was pink. I don't know whose idea it was, but it looked lovely; imagine a pink sofa, a pink toilet, a pink telephone and pink door handles.

Just don't ask if the spoons and forks were pink; I don't know, I never saw any forks or spoons at Polina's house. We never ate there.

I don't know why Polina chose such a colour; perhaps she wanted to fool everyone. Her soul and mind really weren't pink; it's more likely that they were a bitter purple. I saw that clearly; you can't fool me that easily.

Polina looked like a stain in her apartment. One stain was more than enough for one apartment, which is why I felt like I needed to dress in pink whenever I went to her house. I had never owned anything pink in my life, so I always felt like another stain in Polina's apartment, just not one that was as bright and beautiful as she was.

That evening the French horn player decided to go to Polina's as well. He didn't like Polina; he used to say she was too beautiful. I had to agree, she really was too beautiful, but that wasn't something you could change. You simply had to live with it.

The French horn player did not seem in the least surprised when he entered Polina's apartment; either he was colour blind or it wasn't his first time there. Later it turned out that I was right; he even knew where the cards were. We needed the cards because Polina knew how to tell fortunes. I know a little bit myself, but she knew how to do it better. She told my fortune first.

"Soon you will meet the man of your life," Polina said, barely looking at the cards.

"That's nothing. I meet them every other month." I was unsurprised.

"But this one will be *the one*," Polina said.

"All of them are *the one*." I wouldn't back down and Polina stopped arguing.

"This one will be dark haired," Polina continued.

"Yes, hair colour is important," I agreed.

"One evening, you'll say a fateful phrase. It will be a metaphor, but he won't understand it," Polina said. "Is it important to understand metaphors?"

"Yes, it is," I said.

"And would you leave a man just because he doesn't understand a metaphor?" Polina asked.

"Yes, I would. Just for that," I said.

Polina was silent.

"So I'll leave him, right?" I didn't like ambiguous prognostications.

"Unfortunately the cards show only questions, not answers," said Polina.

The French horn player didn't want his fortune told. I wouldn't have wanted mine told either, had I known how it would all end up.

Afterwards we played hide and seek. One of us would hide a pink glass ball while the other two had three minutes to find it. It's not so easy to find a pink ball in a pink rubbish heap. We were allowed to ask for clues, but we could only ask yes or no questions. We didn't ask many; questions only confused things, it was better to simply look. If we found the ball, the one who had hidden it would lose and as a penalty they would have to kiss the other two players. If the ball was not found, the two looking for it would lose and they would have to kiss the one who had hidden it. And so we played all night, and everyone was happy, because nobody felt as if they had lost.

The easiest way to predict the future 1
or,
Usually the News doesn't
tell us anything new.

Months that begin on a Sunday always have a Friday the 13th.

IT'S NOT hard to tell the future. You simply have to accept that there won't be anything new in the future; nothing that we haven't already seen.

Essential differences
or,
Usually we like those who love us.

I MOVED in with the French horn player the second week after I met him. His apartment was not on the first floor. That was essential.

When I look in the mirror, I notice that I am ugly. For some reason others don't see this. But I am ugly and I don't know what to do about it. I close my eyes, but inside my eyelids the mirror is still there – I still see myself. I dislike ugly people; I never wanted to be ugly. At least others can't see that I am; I don't want to subject others to ugliness.

The French horn player said that I had beautiful skin and I was glad because I have more skin than eyes or legs. That's why he caressed me so much; beauty is something people want to touch, like water or sand. The French horn player said that my skin was creamy. I don't know what he meant by 'creamy', but I think most people's skin is creamy. He also said that my skin was as soft as silk; I liked the idea that my skin had been made by spiders and worms. They made it for themselves, not for me; I took it from them and wore it as if it were my own.

Often he would lean towards me and when I pulled away, he would say, "Don't be afraid. I only want to smell you." I couldn't help pulling away; in my head if you like something, you should run from it. Being smelled was nothing. The problem was that when I pulled away I spilled my coffee or was dusted with ashes.

Dust and ashes. Ashes and vines. His hands were like vines, trained to hold the French horn firmly. That's how firmly he held me, and I liked it. You feel different when you're being held, compared to when you're not. Take the wind, for example, it isn't held by anyone and what's the good in that? When nobody is holding me, I say anything that comes into my head. One time I even said there was nothing wrong with murder. Nobody agreed with me, but I'm sure everyone has wanted to do it at least once, they just don't want to talk about it. But everyone likes to listen to what others have to say. And the wind kills. If not, then why does it blow so fiercely?

The French horn player's bedding was striped. I don't like striped bedding. If you lie across the bed, the stripes tell you you're not behaving correctly. I liked everything else in his apartment, and I think that if you like something you should say so.

"I like your apartment," I said.

"So buy it," the French horn player offered.

If a man offers to sell you his apartment, it's a sure sign he's in love with you.

Three is always better than two
or,
Usually the things we talk about are of no interest to ourselves, much less to anyone else.

AFTER OUR night of fortune telling, the three of us were together almost all the time, except for those evenings when Polina and I pretended that we didn't know each other or when the French horn player had to play somewhere. (I never asked if the woman with colourless eyes played with him. You don't need to know everything).

We argued constantly. I never knew there could be three completely different opinions on every question. For example, after watching a film I said I didn't like the protagonist.

"How did you know which character was the protagonist?" asked the French horn player.

"The protagonist is the one with the most screen time," I said.

"I think they're the one whose actions most affect the plot," said Polina. "For example, a lover or a murderer."

"No, the protagonist is the protagonist's mother, because if it weren't for her, there would be no protagonist," said the French horn player.

"What mother? There were no mothers in the film," I disagreed.

"Or perhaps the protagonist's child," the French horn player paid no attention to me. "Maybe he'll achieve more in his life than the protagonist."

"Or perhaps somebody the child will meet much later in life," I agreed.

Polina ordered another coffee. The waitress asked us politely to speak more softly, because she couldn't hear what her other customers were ordering.

One time I noticed the French horn player holding Polina's hand. He didn't let go even when he caught me looking. For a few moments, I felt as useless as a piece of rubbish, but when the French horn player finally let go of Polina's hand, the feeling passed. Only then did I notice that they were sitting together and I was on the other side of the table. That's how we always sat and this had never seemed odd to me. I like to sit facing the people I like.

Conformism

or,

Usually people don't know what's good for them; they need to be told.

Conformism (Lat. Conformis "similar") – a moral and political concept, conferring an accommodating attitude, an avoidance of expressing one's own opinion, an uncritical attitude. This is a defensive reaction, one that seeks to undermine the opposition between an individual and an asocial sense of self.

HERE ARE ten random, but relatively common professions: a train conductor, a French horn player, a cosmonaut, an art critic, a dentist, a pimp, president, an actor, an elephant trainer, and a kiosk attendant. Try to determine which of these match best. I would organize them as follows (I've noted what these professions have in common in parentheses):

French horn player and elephant trainer (sound)
Train conductor and art critic (peace and stability)
President and pimp (concern for others)

Dentist and actor (exaggerated passions and a constant
    uncomfortably stooped pose)
Cosmonaut and kiosk clerk (tight working quarters)

I think that people living as a couple need to have similar
professions. The more alike they are, the better they are likely
to understand one another. If people aren't similar, they will
try to be in every possible way, and that's terrible.

The French horn player was a French horn player, and
Polina was a lawyer. Besides that, he was a man, and she, a
woman. He was white; she was black. I couldn't see any
points of convergence. Someone should have told them that
they were incompatible.

That's probably what I wanted to tell them when I
followed them that night. I'd been living back at my house
for a week, so I wasn't in a hurry to go anywhere. Polina
was carrying a sequined purse and the French horn player
was lugging his horn. Once in a while they'd stop and kiss.
I didn't like that. (The French horn player and I never
kissed in the street. Which was a pity.) At least one of his
arms was occupied so he couldn't hold her in both arms.
Because the kisses were half-hearted, they weren't as hurt-
ful. The horn, it seemed, was more important to him,
since he wouldn't put it down even when he was kissing
her.

When they stopped to kiss yet again, I wanted to make a
snowball and throw it at them, but there was no snow. And
besides, I didn't want them to see me.

I'm not sure if I didn't like them, or if I hated them; I
needed to decide, because the difference between these two

states is not just quantitative, but qualitative. People only do something if their emotions are very strong.

I did something. I wanted to know if they really were in love with each other. I could think of only one surefire method – if they heard a sound and turned to look, that would mean that there wasn't the slightest whiff of love between them. But if they wouldn't stop kissing, then there was no mistaking it; we could all forget about them and let them be.

When they finally stopped kissing, I sneezed. Then once again more loudly. Even though I was close enough for them to hear me, neither turned. I couldn't shout "help!" because they would have recognized my voice. Besides, it would have been impossible for them to save me from themselves.

As I tried to get their attention, a shot was heard (perhaps it wasn't a shot, but it sounded like one) along with the sound of glass shattering. That was fate offering me a helping hand, using the most unexpected measures. Polina and the French horn player jumped away from each other (I'm pretty sure that real lovers don't behave like that), and hurried away, forgetting to hold each other's hand. So I still had some hope. When I saw them, I would tell them.

The Egg

or,

Usually the bigger the egg,
the harder the shell.

I DON'T know about you, but I like to dream that someone's chasing me. I run as fast as I can, so he can't catch me, but still I can't escape. The shadow can't catch up with me; it lags several metres behind. He exudes a pleasant warmth. Sometimes the shadow extends his arm and touches my back. My whole body quivers to his touch and I hear a quiet, calm music.

I want to turn back to see how he looks, but he won't let me. The whole time he's speaking, but I can't understand a thing. His voice calms me. If he hits me, I feel no pain; if he deceives me, I'm not sad.

If I wanted to have sex with him, I sense that I could at any time. But I don't actually want to – it's enough to know that he wants it. To know that if I touched his hand, he wouldn't draw it away, if I sat next to him, he wouldn't move. He loves me not just with his soul, but with his body, as if I was a living thing that's pleasant to take in your hand.

I dream that he wants something, but doesn't ask, and I have to guess. I dream that he's stepping on my toes, as if he wanted to knock me down. But I am in control, and whenever I want to, I can push him away.

Only at the end of the dream did I understand why I was not getting anywhere. The reason I kept hitting against something was because I was inside an egg. A large, static egg, its white not transparent enough for me to see through, its yolk a yellowish red. As I dreamt, I imagined that it was the sun. I've heard that the reddening sun is beautiful so I had no reason to be suspicious. I would have been disappointed to learn that it was not the sun, but an egg yolk, even if it was suspended somewhere beyond out beyond reach.

I would be disappointed, but it's important to recognize that this dream was no metaphor. There was no deeper meaning and I would never hatch from the egg. There are plenty of eggs from which nothing ever hatches.

One night

or,

Usually it's best not to desire. That way you never have to fight.

SUCCESS COMES mostly, I think, from persistence. (For example, as a child, I tried to grow a sunflower from roasted sunflower seeds and after many attempts, I succeeded.)

That's why I followed them every night.

But one night I got hit by a car and I died.

A molecule
or,

Usually love at first sight dies the minute you direct your gaze elsewhere.

*Atoms typically combine into molecules. A molecule
is the smallest part of a substance that can exist
by itself. For example, an oxygen molecule is
made up of two combined oxygen atoms.*

THE NEXT morning, I woke up in a much better mood.
I didn't shower; I never do when I'm in a good mood. Why
shower when there is nothing to wash away?

I knew I loved him. I can't live alone. My neighbour lives
alone and I see what loneliness has done to her; she's let
herself go and it's made her happy. She doesn't wash her hair,
she's always smiling and she never complains about anything.
She has a husband, but he has been in prison for a long time.
Many years ago he tried to kill her with an axe, and although
she defended him to the best of her ability in court, the crack
in her head was just too big. I don't know if this is the truth,
because there's no scar on my neighbour's head. And there's
no husband. My neighbour waters her plants and keeps her

eye on everyone, but she doesn't stick her nose into anybody's business.

I don't want to be like that. That's why I believe in love at first sight. I believe in love that begins even before you've seen your beloved. For a while you feel that you love some-one, but you don't yet know who. You have to take a good look around. I took a good look. There was a very attractive person standing in our courtyard. At first I couldn't tell if it was a man or a woman. The figure had a shaved head and was holding a box in their hands. And, although the figure was wearing a skirt, for some reason I suspected it was a man.

It was early morning. Still dark. The person was fumbling at my neighbour's door. At first I thought it was my neigh-bour, because although the figure was taller, it looked a lot like her.

"Are you looking for something?" I asked.

"None of your business," answered the person, unlocking the door and disappearing inside.

I leaned over to take a look and almost fell off the balcony. I spilled my coffee on myself, but saw nothing. Putting on my glasses, I leaned down again. Nothing. From my neigh-bour's apartment, I could hear the melancholy voice of a man. It was sad in a pleasant way. Though the voice was asking something, nobody responded. I walked downstairs, went up to the neighbour's door and crouched down to look through the keyhole, when the door opened unexpectedly.

"I'm Alex," the person said.

"So what?" I said.

"Is it eight already?" Alex asked.

"I don't know," I said, but he was looking at me as if he didn't believe me, so I repeated, "I don't know."

I took off my glasses, wanting to look prettier. But I doubt Alex noticed this.

Pandora

or,

Usually people don't take what they are given and don't run when they are attacked.

I DOUBT that:

- time moves constantly forward in an orderly fashion.
- time is going to end sometime (that would mean that at some point there will be no time. Everything that ends must have had a beginning).
- time even exists. Just because we count something doesn't prove anything. We count gods, but that doesn't mean they exist.

Alex looked at his watch again.

"What's in the box?" I asked. I'm not sure that I really cared or if I simply wanted to get his attention.

"The same as what's usually in boxes," Alex answered.

Buttons or letters, I thought. Why carry them around?

"Can I take a look?" I asked.

"What do you mean? It's Pandora's box, you had better not open it."

Pandora was probably his mother, I thought. (At the time I thought it an odd name). Mothers often pass on all kinds of boxes of inheritances to their children. On several occasions, later, I addressed my neighbour by this name, but she never responded. This didn't surprise me. My neighbour never showed the slightest interest in her neighbours.

"I fancy a cup of coffee." Alex smiled.

"I don't drink coffee," I answered rather brusquely, because I didn't like the irony in Alex's voice.

"If you're going to lie, at least change your clothes." Alex laughed and glanced out into the street again. He took me by the hand as if for the tenth time, and repeated calmly, "I'd love a cup of coffee."

I hated the sound of that "love". I don't like people who are presumptuous.

"I'll get changed," I said softly, thinking he wouldn't hear. I didn't want him to let go of my hand.

"It doesn't matter," Alex said. He took me to the nearest café, but I began to grumble that I didn't like the place, though it didn't make any difference; after all, what does it matter where you get your coffee? I just wanted to walk with him a little longer.

Alex told me that my neighbour was his mother; they hadn't talked for ages, he said, but it didn't matter because they understood each other without words. A mother and son's relationship is always special.

"Why haven't I seen you before?" I asked Alex.

"Because you were blind and now you have learned to see." Alex kissed me again. I don't know how many times he kissed me, because it seemed so normal and natural, that I didn't even think of counting. I'm glad I'd taken off my glasses; they would have got in the way when we kissed. I'd have had to take them off and toss them aside to free up my hands. I always try to keep my hands free. I like to be ready, so that if I ever meet anyone unexpectedly and want to throw my arms around them, I can.

The whole time Alex kept hold of his box.

"Why don't you leave it at your mother's?" I asked.

"My mother doesn't want it," Alex answered.

I couldn't understand what it was about that box of buttons or letters that bothered my neighbour, perhaps it was just that once you give something as a gift, you want the person to take it not leave it behind as if it was unimportant. When you give a gift, you want someone to cherish it.

"Once I read a book about a black girl who dreamed of having blue eyes, imagining all that she could achieve if she had them," I said as we drank coffee.

"Did the book have a happy ending?" Alex asked.

"How could a book like that end happily?" I couldn't understand.

"Maybe she got blue eyes."

"No, she didn't."

The whole time Alex kept hold of my hand. I don't know why, I had no intention of running away. It didn't matter what he did. But he had no way of knowing that.

Sombra*
or,
Usually a single object can have several shadows.

Shadow – a tract of darkness which light rays cannot illuminate because of an obstruction to their path. Historically, before clocks were invented, shadows were used to tell the time. This is impossible at the Poles; because of the sun's position there, the length of shadows does not change over the course of a day.

EVEN THE thinnest strand of hair has a shadow.

From that day on, I became his shadow. You don't get to choose whose shadow you'll become, or when. It's fate. I don't know why you would think that being a shadow is a bad thing, I actually like it. Of course, a shadow can't exist without its master. But I didn't feel the need to exist all of the time. In the evening, when it's time for Muslims to say their third prayer, the shadow becomes twice as large as its object.

---

*   Spanish – shadow

I loved Alex, but I never told him. I think that you can only tell a person that you love them if you have absolutely nothing else to say to them.

"I like books with happy endings," said Alex. "Not too long ago I read a chess manual; in chess the white pieces always start and always win."

"And the black pieces?"

"What about the black pieces?" asked Alex.

"Does anything good happen to them?" I didn't understand.

Alex didn't answer. It wasn't important; a person couldn't possibly have an answer to every question.

It was Alex's own fault that I became his shadow; he put me in that situation. He never loved me; he always looked right through me, as if I were not there. He would hold my hand and caress it as if he didn't really believe that I was real. He would continually ask me questions, probably thinking that if I were to stop talking, I would disappear. He never called me by my name. But that's normal; shadows don't have names.

(One evening, a wolf was crossing the plain. The sun was low in the sky and the wolf's shadow grew long. The wolf thought, "I've got nothing to fear, if I had a shadow 30 meters long, I'd be the king of the beasts. At that moment a lion appeared; the lion pounced on him, mauling him to death.)[*]
The same day, Alex bought me a watch, as if it were my job to help him keep time.

---

[*]   Aesop's fable

"What's this watch for?" I was angry. I had no desire to wear something on my wrist. I didn't want him to give me anything. I have never understood what people expect when they give me gifts.

"So that next time I ask if it's eight, you'll know," Alex said.

I didn't ask him why he couldn't wear a watch himself and check it when he needed to.

"It's a ladies' watch anyway," Alex said.

"I get that there can be feminine and masculine eyes, but a watch is a watch. How can it be feminine or masculine? Does it mean that time has a gender too?" I was angry, but I realized it was pointless.

From then on, whenever he wanted to know the time, he looked at me. I didn't like it. I wanted him to look at me just for the sake of it, without any purpose, not needing anything. But it was never like that. He only needed me to help him carry out his secret mission (secret even to himself): to take care of his little box.

Not-Alex

or,

Usually the recognition of human dignity and equal and inalienable rights is the foundation of freedom, justice and peace in the world.*

DON'T READ books. Why do you need to know or feel something that never was and never will be? There's no such time; there's no such place.

I'd like to be a man; walk like a man, laugh like a man, see the world like a man. I would like to be one of the men I've loved.

People are not perfect. To be perfect you would have to be made of all 103 chemical elements outlined in the Periodic Table. Alkalines are important, as are the lanthanides, and the inert gases. Perfection for human beings, therefore, is elusive. I don't know why God made us this way. He created the thief who has to spend his whole life trying not to be one.

But individuals are not the issue. Individuals do not exist. The only thing that exists is the love or hate that is produced by their interaction.

---

* From the Preamble to the Universal Declaration of Human Rights

I went for a walk with Alex. He walked faster than I. I hurried, not wanting to fall behind. We walked fast. We were probably in a hurry to get somewhere.

"Why are your shoes dirty?" Alex asked.

"I don't know," I said. "Everyone's shoes are dirty."

"Everyone who has shoes, has dirty shoes," Alex said.

"Yes," I said. Talking was difficult; we were walking fast and on top of that I was smoking.

"I'd like to open a shoe rental shop," Alex said.

"Ugh, it would be disgusting to wear a stranger's shoes."

"People often do disgusting things."

We stopped. Alex decided to buy me flowers. I said I didn't need flowers. He said I could throw them out if I didn't need them and bought me red ones. Carrying flowers around that had been grown in a greenhouse for someone's pleasure disgusted me as much as wearing a stranger's shoes. I threw them into the first rubbish bin we passed, but Alex paid no attention.

It seemed to me that we were walking in circles. When I asked, Alex said, "Yes, that's how it is. But we don't walk in circles. We walk in cycles."

"I've never understood the difference between circles and cycles," I said.

"The more things are similar, the harder it is to understand the difference between them," Alex explained.

When someone explains something to me, I usually understand better. Alex was good at explaining things. He drew two perfectly similar circles on the ground and said that one was a circle and the other, a cycle. And then he asked if I knew which one was which.

"Of course," I answered. You only have to want to understand and everything makes sense.

I looked up from the circles and saw something I had no desire to see. Straight ahead of us, a man was walking along the street. He was the exact image of Alex. For a moment I thought it was his reflection in the mirror, but it wasn't possible because this other man, Not-Alex, walked without me at his side, and he wasn't carrying the box.

"My God, you are so beautiful!" Not-Alex said as he approached us.

From this I concluded that either he was blind, or he had no idea what beauty was. Later he told me that he fell in love with me the moment we met, but I never believed him.

For many years, he told me, he had loved nobody else, only me. When I would tell him that he had to stop loving me, he would say, "I can't stop loving you just because you tell me." I think he could have done if he had tried.

I understood immediately that this meeting did not bode well. I wished I hadn't met him, but there was nothing I could do. He had a right to walk the same streets as Alex.

The easiest way to predict the future 2
or,
Usually it's not so cold.

The lowest possible temperature is -273 C. This is called absolute zero. At this temperature all the thermal energy of atoms and molecules vanishes and thermal radiation stops.

IT'S NOT hard to predict the future. You only have to accept that one day the future will never come.

A shadow has no lips

or,

Usually what we want has nothing to do with what we do.

SOMETIMES THE distance between people is large, but crossed easily. Sometimes that space is tiny, but impossible to cross. By any means. I loved Alex. I spent hours with him, but he never seemed close to me, it was as if he was on the other side of a curtain. I wanted to draw the curtain open, but he didn't. I couldn't ask. After all, a shadow has no lips.

And even though I didn't like it, Not-Alex became, instantly, my heart and soul. From the first moment I understood him and knew him better than myself. I knew where he would go and what he would do, what he felt and what he wanted. I didn't love him in the slightest; I felt him. Neither of us understood why this was, why it was so easy to be together. We asked Alex, but he said that it was no business of his. Alex didn't care that I loved him, but lived with his brother.

Yes, I lived with Not-Alex for five months. I had completely forgotten about this period in my life. Not-Alex was the first man who ever agreed to live with me. It was odd to find another body in my bed every morning. I don't know if his soul was there too. It probably was, but I didn't care. I can't love two people at the same time.

I don't think there will ever be an apocalypse. I think that we'll live for eternity; I hope I'll live alone.

Not-Alex was always smiling. He smiled when he was awake, and even when he was asleep. He told me about how, when he was little, he always knew that his mother loved his brother, not him. (I wanted to tell him that unfortunately I was no different). Whenever Not-Alex played the piano as a child, his brother would sneak over and slam the cover shut. Usually Not-Alex failed to move his fingers away in time. His mother would say, "Why the devil do you need to practice day in and day out? Don't practice, and then you won't have to complain." Or, when he'd fall asleep, his brother would wake him. Then his mother would say, "You'll have plenty of time to sleep the rest of your life." When he would take a bath, his brother would hold his head under water and let go only when Not-Alex had begun to turn blue. "Nobody is forcing you to bathe together," his mother would say. One time, when he was asleep, his brother shaved his head, then he pelted him with a dead bird he had found, until it fell to pieces.

That's when Not-Alex began to smile. At first out of love, then out of sadness, out of loneliness and later out of habit. I don't know if this is the truth, but that's how he told it. He seemed utterly disposable to me, like a large, fully absorbed teabag in a cup.

I had no doubt, then, why his mother had given the box to Alex.

Not-Alex was not handsome, but I couldn't keep my hands off of him. It was only later, when we were no longer living together, that I understood why I always stood so very close to him; he radiated a simple and not unpleasant happiness.

I wonder if my closeness annoyed him. I thought it was smart to stand very close; that way he could not see how ugly I was. Close up, my features blur, it's impossible to see the details.

Being with Not-Alex, I felt warm and calm. Don't ask what we talked about, because I don't remember. Maybe beauty, or maybe self-destruction. I would press against him and it felt good. But I saw only Alex. Alex behind a curtain, which I couldn't draw open. I couldn't kiss him, because I didn't have lips.

Tell me

or,

Usually people know a lot.

TELL ME what you know about

- water, which does not cleanse and dust, which does not provide cover
- schisms, secessions, *coup d'états* and anarchy
- the lives of insects in stagnant water
- blossoms, the very bluest of all known blossoms
- disorders of the temporomandibular joint
- a parrying (blocking an opponent's attack or deflecting it) weapon, suitable also for attack
- purification (removal of impurities)
- the Id
- geometric progressions
- the goddess of love, passion, and blooming fields
- birds of the raptor species, with strong hooked beaks and sharp-taloned claws
- wave guides and breakwaters

. . . and I'll tell you who you are.

Liar. Cover.

or,

Usually what we want has nothing to do with what we get.

I CAN'T justify what I did as an accident. I wanted to do it, and I did it. And if I feel like it, I'll do it again.

Not-Alex was at work. He was a women's Taekwondo teacher. He taught little girls, pretty ladies, and middle-aged women to kick. I'm not sure this could be actually be classed as work.

"It's really important for everyone to know how to defend themselves," Not-Alex would argue.

I agree, but I just don't understand why it's more important for women to defend themselves than men. Or why Not-Alex never defended himself against his mother and brother.

I only visited Not-Alex at work once, but that was enough for me to fall in love. Not with Not-Alex, but with her. She wasn't young, or pretty, or thin. She had been studying with Not-Alex for five years, but hadn't learned a thing. She was married with three grown-up sons and an older husband who was a lawyer. She was a lawyer herself, defending everyone from everything.

I was waiting for Not-Alex, which is why I had time to have a cup of coffee with her. She just came right out and invited me.

"Do you have time to get a coffee?"

"Yes," I answered, though I thought it a little strange that someone would start chatting with me just like that.

"My name is Ana," she said. I would have believed her, but Not-Alex had told me her name was Anastasia. Why would she lie about her name? I considered that perhaps it was a good sign that someone would lie with their first sentence.

"My name is Blanca," I said. And I wasn't lying. It wouldn't have been interesting if I was lying too.

"I've been studying with your husband for five years now," said the lawyer.

"He's not my husband," I didn't say, because that was the first time that anyone had ever imagined I might have a husband. It was only possible for her to make such a mistake because she didn't know me. Or perhaps she said it in order to trick me – who knows? Lawyers, they're clever people. As I said nothing, the lawyer tried again.

On the windowsill a cat was sleeping. I don't like cats sleeping in cafes; I scratched it on its side and it woke up unhappily. Now we were both unhappy with each other, but we hid it from each other. It's always better to pretend that you love everyone.

"I'd rather kick someone than shake hands with them," Anastasia said. (There was nothing unusual about that, I thought; when you kick someone, your victim is farther away and you can't tell how much you're hurting them. It would be better if you could send the blow by post, sealing it in an envelope like a letter. After all, if you can't see the harm you've done, you don't feel you've done any harm.)

For some reason I didn't voice my reply, but this didn't bother her.

"When I was little," she began, and I thought, thank God, everyone was a child once; at least we have something to talk to each other about. For some reason nobody starts their stories in the present. Nobody says, "When I was precisely the age and state of beauty and mind as I am now . . ."

I don't know if my train of thought was too long, or whether Anastasia's story was very short, but I didn't hear a bit of it. She had finished and was ordering another coffee. I sensed somehow that she wanted to explain why she needed to learn self-defense. I wondered how much coffee she would have to drink till she plucked up the courage.

"I can't stand myself," Anastasia said out of the blue. "I'm trying to learn how to hurt myself."

"Pacifists would say that whatever the situation, whether in war, or just between individuals, an act of violence, even if it's in self-defense, is morally wrong," I said.

"Well, you can tell those pacifists there's no law against acting against oneself in a morally questionable way," said Anastasia. I think she knew better than I what was legal and what was not.

In other words, I fell in love with her because she was crazy (perhaps since her childhood – I don't know; maybe I should have listened to her story). And as well as that, she was working hard; in order to jump, turn 180 degrees at an angle and then hit her target (i.e. herself) was not easy.

"Do you want me to tell you a story?" Anastasia asked slowly.

Why wouldn't I?

"Once upon a time there were nine camels. Between them they had fifteen humps," Anastasia said. "They were all brothers and sisters and their mother had taught them to share everything. So, when the camels walked through the desert, the single humpbacks died before the double humpbacks."

"They didn't share their emergency supplies?" To be honest, I didn't understand the story.

"Of course not. Sometimes even contrary to what you've been taught, sharing simply isn't possible."

The cafe was badly lit. The crooked, modern lamps threw their light in only one direction; Anastasia was perfectly lit, while I sat in complete darkness as if I were not there.

Not-Alex was at work. I liked the fact that he didn't have a set schedule; he worked when they needed him. Someone would call and Not-Alex would go to work. He'd get up and go out, dropping everything he had been doing before the phone call. I like it when people know how to leave things behind.

Not-Alex didn't move all his things to my place. Everything he brought fit into one suitcase and he kept it locked and stowed away behind the sofa. One day when I didn't have anything to do I decided to go through his things. I opened the lock easily with a pair of scissors; it was his own fault – he should have bought a proper lock.

Packed in the suitcase were a range of items; several old, frayed T-shirts, on one of which was written, "He who tries, wins." And on one of the others, written in the exact same font, "Rhinoceros and Hippopotamus: Not exactly the same, but the difference is slight." There were more clothes, a pair of sunglasses (with the logo, "Sun for Fun"), an ugly purple umbrella, a couple of books (*The Brothers Karamazov* and *The Easiest Way To Find the Easiest Way*) and some other rubbish. There was something written on every item, perhaps even on the umbrella; I don't know, because I was too lazy to open it up and check. There's never anything interesting written on umbrellas.

I never saw Not-Alex use any one of these things and I wondered if the suitcase was his. At the bottom of the suitcase there was something wrapped in brown paper. On it, written in tiny letters, were the words, "Bread, Cake, Cake, Cake" (it seems reasonable to assume that the person who wrote this preferred cake to bread). I unwrapped the paper and found the box. Yes, Alex's box.

I had no doubt Not-Alex had stolen the box. Why was he hiding it?

I called Alex and told him I had found his box and that I wanted to meet him to return it. Alex had no idea what I was talking about, but I convinced him to meet me.

That evening I could have sworn Not-Alex was crying. I knew why. Now I was the one who had come over to slam down the keyboard cover. Not-Alex didn't move his fingers away. I woke him. He would have plenty of time in his life to sleep. I dunked him until he became blue. I shaved his head. I pelted him with dead birds. I learned to smile. Which is probably why he ended up staying at my place for another two months.

The snail

or,

Usually the shell can be broken, but you have to crush it with great force.

TIME AND space are only important when you need to meet someone. After you have met them, time and space lose their meaning. Or that's how it seemed to me.

"Tell me what you want, because I don't have much time." Alex was angry.

"I brought your box," I said.

"What box?"

"What do you mean what box? Your box."

"Give me the cursed box; I have to go." Alex's voice was as hard as rock. Probably because the box was cursed; cursed things affect people badly.

"I'll give it to you if you answer three riddles," I said.

"What time is it?" Alex asked. I glanced at the watch he'd given me and told him it was exactly the time it should be. Alex calmed down a little and took my hand. We sat down in the middle of a field. It was neither cold nor hot, neither pretty nor ugly, but I liked sitting next to Alex. He'd agreed to come out, and now he was sitting talking with me. He didn't say that he wanted to go. I allowed myself to think that he must have liked being with me too.

"So, tell me your riddles," Alex said.

"First," I started, but he stopped me.

"Start with the third."

"What is a V8?"

"A spider." Alex laughed.

"Don't be so smug," I said. "It's not a spider at all; it's a v-shaped motor with eight cylinders."

Alex laughed again.

"Tell me the next one."

"Okay. What's MI5?"

"A pumpkin modified five times," Alex said immediately.

"How can you modify a pumpkin five times?" I didn't understand.

"Just like anything else. You modify it and that's that."

"No," I said.

"What do you mean by 'no'?"

"It's the wrong answer!" I said and waved my hands and shook my head. "No, no, no."

"Can I guess again?" Alex asked.

"It's one of the secret services of the UK," I told him proudly.

"Why'd you tell me?"

"Because you can't guess a second time. You just can't."

I lay down; it was nice to lie in a field. Alex also lay down, his head rested next to mine while his body stretched out in the opposite direction, making a long stick out of us. I understand the expression 'every stick has two ends' now.

My feet pointed north; Alex's, south.

I like a light touch.

"Shall I tell you the third riddle?" I asked.

"You already told me the third one," Alex said. "It's enough. Don't tell me any more."

Alex slid a little closer. My head touched his shoulder; his head touched my shoulder. My right ear touched his right ear; his right ear touched my right ear. I couldn't look up, the sky was too blue. Turning my head to the side I kissed his ear and his neck. Alex smiled.

A snail slid across the top of the box, leaving a trail of slime behind. I don't like snails; they're too slow, too well protected, too clever. I flicked it off with my toe.

"Are you listening to what I'm telling you?" Alex asked.

"No," I said.

The snail tried to slide onto the box again, this time from a different corner, as if one slimy trail wasn't enough. I tried not to look.

Alex, unmoving, continued to smile. I unbuttoned his shirt. I caressed and kissed the skin that I could reach. I didn't want to lie next to him. Because of the awkward position, Alex's body looked different. With my eyes closed tight I couldn't even be sure where I was touching him.

Even through closed eyes I could see how attractive Alex was, and how blue the sky was, and how irritating the snail sliding across the box was.

Alex sat up. I shuddered; I hadn't been expecting him to get up so suddenly. I remained stretched out with my eyes closed. Let him go if that's what he wants, I thought. But he wasn't going anywhere. He lay down again, this time with his head on my stomach. Again I couldn't reach anything.

A feeling of bliss washed over me. The bliss of desire. The bliss of surrender.

When I bent down to pick up my things, I saw the snail again. The same one, I'm sure of it – just as slow, just as sneaky, with the same shell. I stepped on it. Deliberately. I listened to it crackle. It deserved it. I pressed my foot down hard and this time the crackle was softer. You never know if their shell will harden again and grow back. I put all of my weight down on that foot. It was my left foot; I remember clearly. This time there was no crackle, only stickiness. I stood there for a while. I didn't rub my foot; I didn't hop up and down; I simply waited patiently. The wind was warm. Carefully, I cleaned my foot and put on my shoes.

Frost

or,

Usually we don't like our own name.

Frost: Ice crystals are formed during fog. They coat tree branches, power lines, etc. Frost crystals are formed by the deposition of water vapor from saturated air, when there is a light wind and the air temperature is lower than -15 °C.

ANASTASIA CAME to *France* every day, which I found annoying. Yes, it's true that I was in love with her, but that didn't mean I wanted to see her all the time. Besides, she frightened the café's patrons: at three o'clock exactly she would do a headstand for five minutes. Inversion poses, she would say, are healthy. Even she, though, didn't know why she had to do this precisely at three o'clock. Anyway, she used to argue, there's no law that says you can't stand on your head in a café.

There was something about her that I didn't like. She walked around in a daze, as if she were lost in a fog, though her profession obliged her to be focused. But you can't hide fog. A frozen state of bewilderment had formed upon her like hoarfrost, and with every movement it flaked off all around her. Not everyone appreciated this; most people find it hard enough to tolerate their own hoarfrost.

Besides, I didn't like her fingers. They were hard, strong, and bony; they gripped onto things. Only old people have fingers like that. (As they grow old, they need to grab hold of everything with an ever tighter grip, as if by doing so they can keep themselves from disappearing.) The lawyer didn't look old. She maintained herself beautifully, with lovely, smooth skin. But fingers never lie.

It wasn't possible to simply chat with Anastasia; all of our conversations were strained. It was interesting to talk to her, but I could barely understand a thing she said. I couldn't answer her questions. For example, she would ask why people thought badly about themselves, or why everything gets better after dark. How would I know?

Anastasia hardly drank. She would sit and gaze around her, or she would talk with Greek. To tell the truth, Greek was no Greek; he didn't even look like a Greek. His real name was Hogarth Hofmannsthal, but I never heard anyone call him that. Greek was a handsome man; a little on the short side and of an indeterminate age.

I think he was about 60, but he was still good looking. He had muscular arms, nice nails, and his eyes – his eyes were a beautiful deep brown while his hair was silver. He was the owner of *France*; he bought the restaurant from some Greeks, along with all its furnishings and the owner's wife, a mature Greek beauty, who loved him very much, but died of some unknown cause just two months later. Greek found himself alone with his restaurant. He changed the name of it, but that was about it. He bought himself a dog, which he also named Greek, but nobody, except for the owner, called the dog by that name. It was constantly stepping on people's toes or lying across the entrance; it never responded to anyone who called it "Greek."

I don't know which of the Greeks Anastasia loved more. She would greet the dog, and then pretend not to see him. But she also pretended not to see the dog's owner. But Hogarth Hofmannsthal was persistent; the minute Anastasia opened the door to the cafe, Greek would shout, "Look who's here!"

As if anyone else cared. In order not to miss her arrival, he hung a little bell above the door, which rang every time anyone opened it. The door would open a thousand times a day; to this day I can't stand the sound of bells.

I enjoyed teasing Greek. Every time the door opened I would shout, "Look who's coming!" But I soon grew tired of this. A few times I pulled the bell down and threw it under a table. I said it broke off itself, but after the third time, Greek fastened it so securely that I couldn't cut it, even with scissors. After that I tried to make myself deaf both to the sound of the bell and to Greek.

But one day Greek crossed the line.

Emptiness is not the same as peace
or,
Usually, just because things move, it doesn't mean something is happening.

IN THE middle of *France* he stood kissing Anastasia. I don't have a problem with that. Let them kiss. I was angry because Greek had strictly forbidden all of us from kissing at *France*; he had even written it into our contracts. To be fair, this was the only term in the entire contract. It was only then that I realized that in the entire contract there was nothing that stated what the owner of the restaurant could or could not do. I didn't think that was right.

Once I saw Anastasia kiss Not-Alex after her workout. Not-Alex didn't seem particularly pleased, but he didn't resist. I stood and watched.

I like the darkness. Eyes give too much away. We are too quick to discard so many things simply because they appear ugly.

What doesn't drown, burns

or,

Usually destruction is creative.

I BURNED *France* down. I don't know why. I took a match and set fire to it.

In the olden days when some long-forgotten hero would fight a giant, hundred-year-old snake nobody else could conquer, he would light a bonfire inside the monster's stomach. I think that was a wise move. As a reward for saving the virgins of the region from death at the jaws of the monster, the hero would receive a princess, a kingdom, and all its wealth. It's possible I wanted a reward too; that's why I burned *France* down.

First the curtains. It was night and *France* was empty. When the curtains were burning brightly, I tried to set fire to the bar, but it wouldn't light. The fire climbed up the curtains to the ceiling, the left side burning better than the right; I wanted it to burn evenly. One curtain was burning while the other was melting; its black drops spattered and sizzled on the carpet which had already begun to smolder.

I stepped back a bit; I had no desire to set myself on fire. The worst thing would have been if my hair caught fire; burnt hair doesn't look good and it smells.

The fire was reflected in the window. I breathed a sigh of relief. Symmetry is always calming.

From somewhere I could hear the sound of music faintly. I hadn't realized the fire would make such a noise. I wasn't sorry about *France*. You can't feel sorry for objects.

I took out a box from Greek's cupboard. Greek kept lost property in it (why must everything be hidden away in boxes?). I could barely lift the box. I opened it to look at what was packed inside; there were some keys, umbrellas, books, shoes, telephones, watches, dogfood, medicine, cigarettes (I took the cigarettes), some nail polish, a plastic bird (I took the bird too), a harmonica (which I took, but then put back), an inflatable pillow, a light bulb, three computer keys (black with the letters x and v, and white with the number 6), two sealed envelopes, soap, and a silver beetle. Why did these things weigh so much? I thought about checking which item was the heaviest, but it was starting to get hot.

I closed the box and placed it closer to the fire. Then I locked the doors and left.

I forgot to check if I'd locked the dog inside.

Incense
or,

Usually the difference between "knowing" and "being certain" isn't significant, except for when "I know" is supposed to mean "I am never mistaken."*

GREEK DECIDED to investigate how *France* had burned down. His inquiries concluded that *France* wasn't set on fire by me; it had burned down by itself. That's what was written in the report. It burned down of its own volition, for no reason at all.

That very same week Greek sold the site of the fire and bought a new café just a few buildings down, around the corner. He washed the soot off the old *France* sign, and nailed it up above the new cafe door. Sometimes it seems to me that I had dreamt it all. The new *France* was identical to the old one, even the same patrons frequented it. I didn't make sense to me that the fire hadn't destroyed their desire to keep doing the same thing over again.

Greek calmed down, but not Anastasia. She thought that it had to have been either Polina (because she hated *France*)

---

* Wittgenstein. *On Certainty*

or Not-Alex (because he was the last to leave the cafe that day, and after he left, he didn't go anywhere. He dawdled by the door, smoked a cigarette, called someone on his phone, and then just loitered there, smoking another cigarette).

Nobody paid any attention to Anastasia.

"Let her think what she wants," Greek said.

We let her.

It was only after the fire that I understood that life is like incense; when nothing is happening, everything is calm and quiet and there is no scent. But just light it and everything starts, everything opens up and crawls out, as if it were just waiting for the opportunity. Some like the scent, some don't, but it exists. You can't shove it back in. Everything else you can, just not the scent.

Having burned down *France*, I realized that:

1. Polina was Anastasia's daughter (Greek told everyone).
2. Neither Anastasia nor Polina would have admitted this, even under torture.
3. Some things in life happen by chance – the streets you walk, the stairs you climb, and the people you live with.
4. And some things that are still unclear.

A ray of light

or,

Usually, once you start something, it's hard to stop.

Ray: A straight line with a beginning, but no end point.

I DON'T like to touch people. I don't like to touch their skin. Skin is as repulsive as snakes are. It's slippery. It's like touching intestines. I prefer people to be dressed. But people like it when you touch their bare skin. If I must touch them, I try to use the back of my hand, not my palm. It's less sensitive.

I lied. Sometimes it's not that disgusting. Sometimes I can tolerate it. People are warm. When you touch them, you understand that things aren't as simple as they appear.

Lots of people came to *France*, but I couldn't tell them apart; they all looked the same to me. A fat lady in a red dress used to come every day. She'd drink nothing but beer and leave just as it began to get dark. I have no idea where she would go after she left. She was obviously lonely. Women who have a man don't wear red. Then there was a blonde girl in checkered jeans, with curly hair. Whenever she would get up to leave, the girl would say in a firm voice, "Goodbye. I'm leaving for good." But the next day she would be back. There was a man in a floral shirt, wearing glasses and an idiotic expression on his face. And there was another man, grey, with a long moustache who looked like a beaver. I liked Beaver; he seemed trustworthy. If Alex hadn't taken the box, and if I had nobody else to give it to, I would have given it to him. He would have known what to do with it.

A lot of lonely people came to *France*, but they never spoke to each other. Each sat at their own table, nursing their drinks, contemplating their lives as if from a distance.

Greek didn't like their sense of isolation. I think he didn't like the fact that all these people were taking up his space. It's important to bring people together, he would say, because similar things bond together more easily. What nonsense.

But Greek had a lot of crazy ideas. He'd order me to take a beer to Red Dress and tell her that Beaver had bought it for her. I'd take it over, scowling. Red Dress would drink the beer, not even glancing in Beaver's direction. But Greek wouldn't give up. He would order me to take more and more beer and other drinks, day in and day out.

When I grew tired of this, I started mixing up Greek's orders. The drinks Beaver was supposedly buying for Red Dress I'd take to Floral Shirt. I couldn't think of anything better to do. But it was completely irrelevant because not a single one of them played along with Greek's games; games that had a beginning, but no end.

For the sixteenth time that week, I deliberately confused the clients that Greek had told me to take drinks to. I got so involved in the game that I began to mix up all the other orders too. They would order one drink and I'd bring another. It was rare that someone objected. I don't know if they were too lazy to argue, or if they simply didn't care what they were drinking.

On one occasion, when I was taking spaghetti instead of a filet of salmon to a cultured, but rather neurotic man, the bell above the door rang. For a long time I had stopped paying attention to it, but for some reason at that moment I turned around.

Alex walked in the door. He was more attractive than ever. He was alone. I'd never seen him with anyone; even when he was with me it had never seemed that he belonged to me alone. I always had the feeling that he was made up of several parts: one part was seated there, another somewhere else (where? He probably didn't even know himself). Alex was like a ray of light. You could see where it began, but it was impossible to make sense of where it ended.

He didn't look in my direction. I felt like I was drowning. Wherever I looked, I saw nothing but sea and sky. I placed the spaghetti on the first table I came to; a small boy happily pulled the plate close and began to eat.

Alex went over to the bar. For a few minutes he waited as Greek didn't pay him any attention. I stood unmoving in the centre of *France*. Alex bought a colourless drink and sat down by the window. He didn't see me. I wasn't surprised. Often I am invisible. I couldn't laugh or cry, but I had to do something. It was now or never.

Going up to his table I asked if he wanted anything. Alex raised his eyes and looked at me. For a long time he looked at me and then said finally, no, he didn't want anything else. I turned and walked away.

This is where the water stops. This is where the tragedy starts. No, I didn't want this kind of life.

He sat with his back to me. I wanted to go up to him and touch his shoulders. His shirt looked thin enough for me to feel the warmth of his skin, but thick enough to prevent me from feeling its softness. I told myself I would count to ten and go. But Alex picked up his drink, poured it into the flowerpot on the windowsill, stood up and left. He left nothing behind.

I stood there, unable to move. What had happened, happened. The present is not perfect, but the future is. Next time I would touch him. If he wanted, I would even touch his skin. After all, people like their loved ones to touch them.

When I look at the mountains I want to cry
or,
Usually things that appear to be big
are in fact small, and vice versa.

PAIN IS tiny; as small as a single cell. Every life is made up
of cells.
Sadness is tiny. That's why you can never know where it is.
The origins of all things are tiny.
I think we should cherish tiny things.

All roads which lead to the kingdom
of the underworld are the same

or,

Usually what never happened to you,
has already happened to others.

I'M USED to having people love me, but I never love them back.

Why do people want so desperately to be loved? Why can't they simply live? I had to leave Not-Alex, because he could no longer bear my not-love. I tried not to show it; I was good to him. But Not-Alex wanted me to belong only to him; he could not accept that it could never be.

I think it's wrong to want people to belong only to you. But there's nothing you can do about it. When you fall in love, that's what happens.

For example, Anastasia loved Not-Alex.

"I will love him no matter what he does," she often said.

Everyone knew this wasn't possible. Nobody can keep loving someone when they do whatever they want.

Let me tell you a story. When I was about fifteen, I fell in love for the first time. I don't remember his name, just that he was freckled and had long blond hair. One night we walked around town for a long time until we came to a bridge. I decided to balance on the railing. "You can do what you want," he said as I started climbing. I kept my balance perfectly well. I didn't give him my hand; back then I wouldn't let anyone touch me.

And then, inexplicably, I fell into the water. It wasn't intentional, but he thought I had tried to drown myself. I only wanted to walk along the railing. And I always did what I wanted. There was no sign anywhere that said walking on the railing was dangerous.

Not only did he refuse to rescue me, but he called the ambulance and the police. Luckily, before they arrived I swam to shore and ran away. He left me the next day, explaining that he wanted nothing to do with a psychopath.

I was still standing riveted to the spot in *France* when Not-Alex walked in. I leaned back against the wall so he couldn't see me. It didn't work. He hurried over and began to kiss me. I stood frozen. With Not-Alex I never had to move. Even if I stood for a year in the same place without budging, Not-Alex would stand next to me and worship me. Truth be told, it's more convenient when idols stay in the same place.

But I wanted to move. I told Not-Alex that by the time I had finished my shift, I wanted him out of my apartment.

Not-Alex was just opening his mouth to say something, when somebody called on his mobile; I don't know who it was, but I am grateful to them. Not-Alex talked for some time. Afterwards, he left without a word.

All good things come in threes

or,

Usually when you destroy the consequences, the cause also disappears. When you destroy the cause, the consequences also disappear.

SOFTLY, ANASTASIA closed the door to *France* behind her. She hoped that Greek wouldn't notice her leave. His irritating habit of following her around was exhausting her. On her way out, she noticed a man pour his drink into a plant pot, stand up abruptly, and leave the cafe.

The man was attractive and somehow familiar. It was only later that Anastasia realized the man was the spitting image of Not-Alex, though better dressed and more relaxed. And perhaps happier, even. Unsure why, Anastasia followed him.

The man walked quickly. It was raining outside, but he did not seem bothered. He carried something under his arm. As the bag became increasingly soaked, it revealed the object to be square in shape. Like a box, thought Anastasia.

Abruptly the man turned the corner and disappeared from Anastasia's view. She quickened her pace and, as she turned the corner, practically collided with him. He stood talking on his mobile. After the call, he put the box down on the pavement by the corner of a house and paused a moment. Brushing back his wet hair, he made another call and talked for a long time, laughing. You only laugh that way with someone you love. Finishing the call, the man walked away, leaving the box lying on the pavement.

Anastasia had no idea what to do. She wanted to call out to him, to tell him he had forgotten his box. But the man walked briskly and was some way away. I'll wait until he's gone, Anastasia thought, and take the box myself.

It began raining harder and grew dark. The street was deserted. Anastasia couldn't imagine what hole people crawled into when it started to rain. She was very close to *France*. She heard Greek arguing with someone and laughing; it was precisely this about Greek that annoyed Anastasia most. If you're arguing, then don't laugh; if you're laughing, don't argue – how often did Anastasia have to repeat this rule she'd made up especially for Greek? Greek took this as a clear indication of her love. After all, you don't criticize someone you don't love.

The worse thing was that the woman Greek was speaking to was also arguing and laughing. What a loathsome woman, Anastasia though. Listening to the detail of their conversation, she realized it was Blanca.

"Loathsome woman," Anastasia said out loud. Raindrops fell into her mouth.

Remembering the box, Anastasia bent down to pick it up, but noticed the man returning. He was walking slowly; he seemed to be cowering. When he drew closer, Anastasia realized it was a completely differently person. It was Not-Alex. Though she saw this, she could not believe her eyes. How often does luck walk right up to you?

Anastasia stepped back. Not-Alex walked straight to the

box. He picked it up and placed it under his arm just as the other man had been carrying it.

Anastasia knew perfectly well that Not-Alex was twenty years her junior, but there was nothing she could do about it. And Blanca didn't seem much of an obstacle.

"He looks at her as if she were a TV set on mute," Anastasia used to say to Greek. "She couldn't care less that he watched her, and he doesn't understand a thing he sees." This seemed to Greek a clear sign of her love. After all, you don't tell secrets to someone you don't love.

Not-Alex was never one to make the first move, but he was completely powerless in the face of Anastasia's advances. They made love only twice. Not-Alex was young and attractive, but frightened and slow. He was not a good lover, but Anastasia didn't care in the least. Just looking at him was enough to make her happy.

Now, as Not-Alex was walking away with the box under his arm, Anastasia needed to make a quick decision; what should she do? Call him back or not?

They made love. Anastasia sensed that Not-Alex and Blanca had fought and saw it as the perfect opportunity to grab him for herself. However, for the first time in his life, Not-Alex's instinct for self-preservation was triggered and without a word he got up from the bed, and, ignoring Anastasia's appeal to stay, or at least, to call, got dressed and went home – to Blanca.

Fly between one and the other
or,
Usually things turn up, then
disappear again, or, they disappear,
then turn up again.

I WAS asleep when the doorbell rang. I knew it was Not-Alex. I was too tired not to let him in. He got undressed quietly and put his arms around me. Before I fell asleep I noticed that Alex's box was on the dresser, but I didn't have the energy to ask where it had come from.

The box was gone in the morning. I wondered if I had dreamed it. Not-Alex was gone too. There was just a letter. A long letter. There's nothing worse than a love letter written by a man you don't love.

Everything in moderation
or,
Usually once you let things get started, they snowball quickly.

NATURE MAKES human beings possible. Humans make love possible. Love makes nature possible.

Nature makes snails possible. Snails create the possibility of choice. The possibility of choice makes nature possible.

Nature makes eggs possible. Eggs make questions possible. Questions make nature possible.

When I fell from the bridge into the water, it was both warm and frightening.

It was relatively early spring so I don't understand why it was warm, (possibly it was autumn – I don't remember precisely), and it was snowing lightly. I fell for a long time before I hit the water. I almost didn't go under, because I hit the water on my stomach. I think I was lying on the water for a very long time until I came to, but that can't be possible. When I regained consciousness, I was being carried by a strong current. I was lying face down in the water; I had not been breathing for a long time. That was my first thought: I have not breathed in a while.

I had no desire to raise my head. The fact that I wasn't breathing didn't worry me. When I began to grow dizzy, I raised my head and took a deep breath. The city lights shimmered before my eyes. I didn't know who I was. I let the current carry me. It was frightening, but warm.

I felt my scarf choking me. With some effort I managed to unwrap it. Then my shoes began to fall off. My clothes, heavy with water, began pulling me downwards with great force. I became uncomfortable, so I started paddling to shore.

When I reached the shore, I realized I wouldn't be able to climb out because the cement embankment was too steep. I swam with the current for a little while longer, getting caught among the rubbish and detritus. I felt no weariness; I wanted nothing – neither to live nor to die. I was happy that for once everyone had left me alone. I lowered my head back down into the water again and stopped breathing.

When I awoke, I was lying on the shore. I couldn't have climbed out by myself, just as I could not have jumped in by myself. The current must have tossed me out, because there wasn't a living soul in sight.

It was neither warm nor frightening on the shore. The snow had grown heavier and I regretted taking my scarf off. I tried to stand up. My entire body ached, and those body parts which were exposed were bruised and bled profusely. I found my mobile in my pocket, but it didn't work. I walked a bit further and sat down on the ground.

When I woke again, I was lying in a hospital room with ugly yellow walls. There were four girls sharing the room with me; each one of them, had, by a variety of methods, tried unsuccessfully to kill herself.

I couldn't convince anyone that all I had wanted was to walk on the railing of the bridge.

Our first gods were created out of fear
or,
Usually a stop sign only means that you should briefly pause.

VULCANOLOGY: THE science that concerns itself with volcanoes, lava, magma, and all related geological phenomena, the explanations for the creation of volcanoes, their structure and formation.

The primary task of vulcanology is to design methods for predicting volcanic eruptions and thus for preventing natural disasters.

HOW CAN you stop what's unstoppable? It's impossible. It's like trying to avoid what's unavoidable.

Anastasia was fourteen when her mother died. Although he lived with them, her father had never been very concerned about Anastasia or any of the other children, so her mother's death meant more freedom for Anastasia. She had always obeyed her mother unconditionally, but not out of fear, out of love. Her mother had always known what influence she had over her daughter, and all the other children had grown up a long time before. That's why, despite her poor health and long illness, she always found the strength to train Anastasia.

After her mother died, Anastasia cut her hair short for the first time in her life, because her mother had never let her do it. For three months she walked around in a daze as if she could not understand what had happened or what she should do next. Her father didn't notice anything unusual in his daughter's behaviour.

A few months later, Anastasia announced that she was pregnant. Which was unexpected. Nobody knew who the father was. Anastasia didn't know herself, or maybe she just would not tell anyone.

Her daughter was born just four days after Anastasia's fifteenth birthday. The baby girl was quiet; her skin was slightly darker. Anastasia never liked her – she found her a nuisance. She could not for the life of her think of a name for her daughter. After six months, Anastasia's father lost his patience and christened his granddaughter Polina and gave her to a childless neighbour who had wanted a baby all her life.

Having done what was right, Anastasia's father died – not from some exotic illness or a global catastrophe, but from common flu. Anastasia was fifteen. She packed her bags, locked the door and left.

Many years had passed when Polina reappeared. Anastasia was a lawyer by then; she had a husband and other children. Anastasia's other children had long grown up and no longer required anything of their mother; they didn't even want to follow her into law. In general they stayed out of her hair. Polina's behaviour seemed silly and inexplicable to Anastasia. After all, if someone leaves you it means that they want to forget you. They don't want you. Why thrust yourself upon them after so many years?

Although she had barely ever seen her mother, Polina was afraid of her and detested her, but she admired her too and wanted to be like her. She successfully qualified as a lawyer, but she could not emulate her mother in other ways; she was a hundred times more beautiful, she was younger and not so dazed and sullen-faced.

Polina had never actually searched for her mother. She accidentally ended up at her firm for her law school internship. Polina believed that her mother had arranged it that way, but when she discovered that her mother had not only not invited her, but that she had in fact tried in every way possible to prevent her appointment, she began to detest and worship her all the more.

Regardless of the fact that both tried to avoid the other as much as possible, circumstances meant that they met up again and again. By some inexplicable coincidence, they associated with the same people, went to the same places, and made the same mistakes.

Despite their differences, they had two things in common: the same last name and an unquenchable inability to be satisfied with what they had. Rejected lovers would think that they'd left them because of some fault. But the single essential fault was their own; they always wanted to be in a different time and different place.

They both always wanted something they did not have. They rarely knew what it was. If they did know, they usually got it, and then they would become unhappy again. Both of them pretended that this was not the case; they pretended to be happy. They both used the same shade of lipstick, and both smoked. Neither loved the man she was living with and neither lived with the man she loved. They would say that this was the impetus that drove them.

If you were to ask them, they would deny everything written here and would provide you with two completely different versions of events. That's because they were both liars. And that was the fundamental condition that made it possible for them to live, to progress. (Any situation that did not require them to lie made them feel that their lives were either stagnant or regressing).

Everything is strange – only time is ours
or,
Usually we (don't) need only one thing.

ANASTASIA NEVER thought about why she didn't love her daughter. It was much more interesting for her to consider why people loved the people they did. Not to love is much too easy and predictable, Anastasia would say. Animals don't love their young, and that's all right. The offspring grow up anyway. And really, have you ever seen a child that didn't grow up? I haven't.

Polina irritated Anastasia. She thought constantly about how to get rid of her daughter, if not forever, then at least for a longer period of time. But she could not think of anything appropriate and that made her even angrier. Having tried a large number of ineffective means, Anastasia went to a fortune teller to ask for advice.

The fortune teller told fortunes with shivers of glass. She told Anastasia to bring her favourite glass item. Anastasia sensed that this would be the last time she would see the object (she thought the fortune teller would simply take it; fortune tellers always take, not only figuratively, but also literally). She thought long and hard about what she didn't mind losing.

She decided to take a goldfish bowl. It was small and round and easy to carry. Long before one of her children had wanted a fish (Anastasia never could remember which child did what. All her children had blurred into one big child, encompassing all the good and bad that had happened to them). The children were long gone, but the goldfish, oblivious, swam still in circles around the bowl. Anastasia never liked that useless fish; its eyes bulged too much and it was much too pretentious calling itself golden, Anastasia would say. So, without a flicker of compassion, she poured the water and the fish into the toilet bowl and demonstratively flushed it down.

But, having brought the goldfish bowl to the fortune teller, Anastasia realised it hadn't been such a good idea after all. It took a good half hour for the fortune teller to break it; she didn't have the right tools. Anastasia couldn't understand how one could be so unprofessional. The fortune teller tried to justify herself, saying it was her hobby, not a job, but this inflamed Anastasia all the more; hobbies are even more serious than work, and you should prepare yourself appropriately.

After a long argument, when the fortune teller could no longer stand Anastasia, without looking at a single shiver of glass and without asking why she had come, the fortune-teller declared that all Anastasia's problems would be solved if only she would recognize that time was her ally and that she should be patient and stop hurrying things. Anastasia grew sad, because she could never be patient nor could she ever do nothing. And that meant that she would not succeed in getting rid of Polina.

To tell the truth, the fortuneteller was no fortuneteller and didn't have a clue about Polina. She understood, however, that Anastasia was in love. You didn't have to be a fortuneteller to see that.

Anastasia began to cry, surprising herself; the last time she had cried had been fifteen to twenty years before when her children had carted all her jewelry out into the courtyard and lost it. She hadn't cried since, because she had never had reason to.

The fortuneteller was not at all surprised by her tears, because every other client cried. The client before her had not cried and that was why the fortuneteller knew in advance that the next client would. She could predict the future relatively accurately even though she was not a fortuneteller.

The fortuneteller felt sorry for Anastasia. She was too rich and attractive to be crying. She felt she had to help her somehow. The fortuneteller didn't know any formulas for attracting lovers. The lover was clearly much younger than the woman. She was too rich and too pretty to be falling in love with some ordinary man, thought the fortuneteller. What could she offer?

While Anastasia cried, the fortuneteller had a thought and suggested that she buy a fish for the goldfish bowl; she thought a goldfish would be best (she had read somewhere that goldfish make all of one's wishes come true, and the woman looked wealthy, so she could easily afford to buy a fish, perhaps even a gold one).

Anastasia agreed that this was a perfect idea, because she understood finally what the fortuneteller was trying to say, "You can never get rid of the things you want to get rid of."

Mix it, give it out, explain
or
Usually we remember the body, not the soul.

FRANCE WAS nearly empty. I have no idea why. It was lunch time; the place should have been packed, but fate had sent *France's* clients elsewhere. Which was good. I could listen freely to Greek's conversation with Anastasia.

Anastasia was more beautiful than usual and she was laughing. I like people who laugh without obvious reason.

I was daydreaming and missed Greek's question, but I caught Anastasia's answer.

"No. I was at the fortuneteller's."

It was obvious she was lying. I can smell a lie from a mile away. But Greek believed her.

"The fortuneteller told me to buy a goldfish, so I did." Anastasia spoke quietly, but I could hear her perfectly.

Only then did I notice that there was a little bag of water on the bar, a goldfish swimming around inside. I liked it right away. Such big eyes, its whole body shimmering – it could well have been made of gold. After all Anastasia was rich enough. She could certainly have bought herself a real gold fish.

I'll tell you a story. Once I had a very rich friend who gave me a real gold fish (I don't remember if it could swim, or not. It probably could). I wore the fish on a chain around my neck until I lost it. I often wonder what the person who found it looked like.

A person's appearance is very important. Try to remember people you have loved and you will only be able to remember what they looked like; not what they talked about.

"Why couldn't we keep it here for a while, at *France*?" Anastasia asked.

That's all we need! I thought. For someone to move in here.

"Of course," said Greek. "Just buy a goldfish bowl and figure out where you want to put it."

I have nothing against fish; I think fish are much better than people or dogs though I couldn't offer an argument to prove it. I like their facial expressions – you can never tell what they're thinking.

I thought it was highly likely that Anastasia had been a fish in her previous life; her face was pleasantly inexpressive – identical to that of the fish. It was impossible to read what she was thinking; she muttered something, leaning directly in towards Greek's ear. I wondered why she was being so coy. But I always tried to be pleasant with her.

"Does your fish have a name?" I asked.

Anastasia looked at me as if I'd asked for the name of the pancake she was eating. Greek liked the idea. He immediately declared a fish-naming contest and suggested we named it "Greek." Nobody objected.

When I looked at Alex's watch a few minutes later, it was 3:30. Anastasia had forgotten to stand on her head – the first time since the day she had started coming.

I wondered why I had wanted to refuse to wear the watch. Looking at it, I felt like I was looking at Alex himself.

Greek had been hinting for a week that he was planning a surprise for us. Nobody expected anything special, because it was pointless to expect something special from someone like Greek. That day the workers delivered a huge painting. Greek ordered us to move the tables and hung the painting in the most visible spot. The painting depicted a beautiful woman beneath an olive tree. The woman would have been enough. What I didn't understand was why it was necessary to paint a thicket around her.

Although Greek claimed he didn't know who she was, everyone recognised that she was the woman who had lived with Greek after he bought the restaurant from her relatives. It seemed that Greek was afraid he would forget what she had looked like.

Nothing is eternal, but some things last
or,
Usually the fight is long, but not eternal, and one side always wins.

SOMETIMES LIFE simply stops, as if it had reached a deadly full stop. That doesn't mean that everyone stops; on the contrary, they keep trying to do something, it's life that stands still.

I was still living with Not-Alex. Anastasia still spent the greater part of her days at *France*. I hadn't seen Alex for two weeks. Every day Greek drank and bragged that he'd started to write a novel. Everyone said it was a great idea, but I didn't understand what was so great about it. Greek said that his novel would be about the fact that nothing is eternal, that some things take a long time. I've read that, I think, in hundreds of novels and I didn't see why it was necessary to write the same thing again. There's nothing in history that hasn't already happened or that hasn't been documented, Greek said. He asked what he should write about. Should he stop writing altogether? I thought that was a perfect idea, but I didn't say anything.

Nor did I say anything when Anastasia declared that she loved Not-Alex. She came up to me and simply said it. I had no idea what she wanted from me, or what I was supposed to do about it. I congratulated her, I think, saying that it was nice to be in love with someone. I truly like it when people fall in love, but it rarely happens.

"I've loved him for a long time now," Anastasia said.

Again, I congratulated her, because loving someone for a long time is even better than loving them for a short time.

"And does Not-Alex know?" I asked.

"He does," Anastasia said calmly. "I think he does."

I wanted to congratulate her yet again, because it's even better if you love someone and that person knows it. But this time I didn't, because I'm pretty sure that to congratulate someone three times in less than a minute isn't normal. Besides, Anastasia might have thought I didn't have anything else to say.

I actually didn't have anything else to say.

"Greek's woman is beautiful." I pointed at the painting. I tried to say it so that it would sound like a question. "She was too old for him," Anastasia said, without looking up at the painting.

The woman did look a bit older than Greek. It's possible that she really wasn't; perhaps the artist just painted her that way. I didn't understand what it meant for one person to be too old or too young for another.

"But beautiful," I repeated.

"Ugly," Anastasia said stiffly. I thought that she wanted to say something else. I suspected that she wanted to talk about Not-Alex some more.

"Give him to me. You don't need him anyway," Anastasia demanded.

When I was a child, I was a hoarder. I couldn't throw anything away. I filled my shelves with out-of-date sweets and toys I no longer played with. Give it to me, you don't need it anyway, my friends, my sister, even my mother would beg. I never gave anything to anyone. Even when the ants ate my sweets, I would keep the wrappers. If my sister ever succeeded in taking something secretly from my room, I'd rummage through her things until I found it and then take it back.

I don't understand why you keep everything, my sister would say. Do you think you'll need all that junk someday? I didn't think that at all. I didn't need any of that stuff and it was obvious that I would never need it. But they were my things and if I had them, I would never give them to anyone else. I didn't care at all that somebody might need them. If for some reason they hadn't secured them, then they would have to learn to do without them. And I had them, so I had to learn to care for them and cherish them even if they were completely unnecessary to me.

That's what I needed to explain to Anastasia, but it would have taken too long. I knew she wouldn't listen, because she grew bored easily. You needed to be as succinct as possible with her.

"No," was the shortest suitable word, and so I said it.

"Just as I thought," Anastasia said victoriously.

That was the first time I ever saw someone ask for something and be satisfied not to get it.

"Sooner or later, you'll give him to me," she added.

That was the first time I fought for something completely unnecessary. Not a sweet or a wind-up teddy bear, but a person. Believe me, there was no difference.

It's important to rest after working
or,
Usually you can choose what you want to look at, and whether you want to look at all.

ANASTASIA TOLD me that she and Not-Alex had made love. She was a terrible liar. I think it's dishonorable to fight using those kind of methods. Just because you're losing you don't have the right to do or say whatever you want. I said nothing. I considered whether I should just stop talking to her altogether. But she refused to budge. She carried on telling me stories, always, "Me and Not-Alex," "Not-Alex and I".

"Buy that fish of yours a gold fish bowl; it will die in that bag." Perhaps I cut Anastasia's story off too brusquely.

"Greek promised to buy one," Anastasia said.

"I don't care which one of you buys it, just buy one as soon as possible. I feel sorry for the fish." It was obvious that it was not the fish that I was angry about. "It can't ask itself."

"That's all I need," Anastasia agreed. "There couldn't be anything worse than a talking fish. As it is everyone blabs and blabs. I wish I could plug my ears."

Anastasia and I never agreed on anything, so why would we agree on something as trifling as a fish?

"I don't think anyone can stop you from doing what you want," I answered.

"So give me Not-Alex." Anastasia began again. Perhaps some mechanism inside her had broken down; like a scratched record, she was starting to repeat the same thing over and over.

I wasn't scratched, so I didn't say "no" a second time. Anastasia must have thought this was her first victory, so she began her "Not-Alex and I" tales again.

I turned and left. I couldn't listen to her. Besides, Red Dress had been waving to get my attention for five minutes. When I went over to her, Red Dress advised me to stay as far away as possible from that loathsome creature. I didn't understand exactly what she was talking about, but I still thought that it was nice of Red Dress to worry about me even though she didn't know me. I thought about befriending her.

When I went over to the bar to pour a beer for Red Dress, Anastasia came up to me again with her demand. I didn't feel like talking to her. I would have preferred to take the beer over to my new friend. But Anastasia didn't let me go so easily.

"We could compromise," she suggested.

I thought she was about to offer me money, but she didn't offer anything. I couldn't really understand the terms of the agreement; if I were to give her Not-Alex, she would give me nothing. I don't know much about contracts, but my intuition told me this one wasn't fair. But Anastasia was a lawyer; she knew better.

Greek returned with a goldfish bowl. The glass bowl was small and round and easy to carry. Without further ado, I filled it with water and released the fish into it. The idiot swam three laps and jumped out. We all rushed over to catch it. Greek moved last.

Anastasia and I crawled around the floor; the fish jumped like a kangaroo. I had no idea fish were so slippery. A couple of times I caught it, but it squirmed away each time. Or maybe I dropped it, because although it was pretty, it was cold and slimy.

Having lost her patience, Anastasia crushed it beneath her foot. The fish stopped flapping around. I threw it back into the goldfish bowl. For a few moments the fish didn't move, but then it came back to life. That was how Anastasia and I saved a life, even if it was only the life of a fish. When I looked at it, I thought the fish was an unusual shape, as if disfigured by Anastasia's shoe, but that didn't hinder it from living a long life – perhaps it lived to be a hundred.

We were both exhausted. We sat down, each facing a different direction. I stared at Greek's woman.

Anastasia looked in the mirror and couldn't believe what she saw. This can't be me, thought Anastasia. So beautiful, so intelligent, and so old.

I never looked in the mirror. I knew everything there was to know about myself already.

Take what you need, keep it for yourself
or,
Usually neither the sky nor the water is blue. That's just how they appear to us.

Natural (public) resources: resources used by many without doing any harm to each other. There is no charge for their use. This is a resource which occurs naturally; it is not manufactured or produced.

IT'S IMPOSSIBLE to even imagine how beautiful my building was. It was green, with a huge balcony, full of all kinds of rubbish – flowerpots filled with flowers, dead for three years, a scooter (I had wanted it badly, bought it, and then didn't want it anymore), some boxes, two old unmatched chairs, each uniquely beautiful, a statue of a blue cat. And there was more – I'm not even sure of the names of all the other things.

One end of the house faced the street, while the other joined another house at an angle. There was no exit; people would enter our yard and get trapped inside like flies in a jar – you could turn in any direction you liked, but there was only one way back, and either you found it or you didn't.

During the day, I would sit on the balcony and watch them stumble about. For some reason people don't like to go back the way they came; they'd rather push their way through any possible gap, just to keep moving forward. I knew there was no way for them to get out, but I wouldn't say anything. I would sit calmly on the balcony, drink coffee, and smoke, or I would pretend to read a book. Let them find out for themselves how perfectly planned our yard was.

Nobody would climb my ladder. Not even Alex. His mother lived directly below me. Every time he went out into the yard, Alex had to walk around the ladder. If it had been me, I would definitely have tried to find out what was on the second floor, at least when there was nobody home. But Alex didn't. He didn't care one bit about the ladder, the second floor, or me. Or perhaps he'd simply forgotten I lived there. It's normal to forget things, isn't it?

Sometimes I would see Alex coming or going to his mother's house, but he never once glanced up at the balcony or at me. So what? Not everyone likes to look around, after all, especially upwards.

One day when Alex was passing I kicked over an old flowerpot, and it fell to the ground. But to no effect. I simply scared away the pigeons. Alex didn't even turn.

I missed him. I wanted him to come over, to call up to me, 'Climb down', and then I don't know what. It would have been enough for him to say just that. I missed him.

Not-Alex never went to his mother's. I think he was angry that his mother hadn't left the box to him. I would have been angry too.

That reminded me that the last time I had seen the box was at my house. I had already got up to look for it when a girl came into the yard. She was unusually tall and thin, with long hair. It was evident that she didn't know where she was going by the way she looked around at the walls and the windows, as if searching for something.

Why am I always on that balcony watching everyone, as if I don't have anything else to do?

Alex came into the yard and walked over to the girl. I couldn't hear what they said; they didn't touch each other, but something told me that it was time I cried.

They left the yard and walked down the street into the distance. I watched them until they disappeared.

I fell back into the water. It's a good job I had nothing in my hands.

II

THE BOOK
OF FAIRY TALES

'Sadly, there is no magic in the world.

*The world is full not of secrets, but of the
sound of squeaking in the ear.'*

Milorad Pavic. *The Inner Side of the Wind,*
or *The Novel of Hero and Leander.*

Do not repeat. There is no need to repeat.
Or,
Usually it's hard to understand
why you fell into the water the
first time. The second time is
even harder to justify.

SWIMMING: ACTIVE or passive motion through the water from the perspective of the water. This differs from drifting (slow movement in air and water) and floating (maintaining of the same depth in air or water).
At this stage you should be able to inhale rhythmically after every two strokes . . . (I know how to breathe rhythmically. I enjoy rhythmic activities.)

For the athletic body this is a bit too often . . . (Too bad! Too often is worse than not often enough).

Inhaling after every four strokes leads to dizziness when you pick up speed . . . (I often get short of breath. I don't know about you, but for me, this happens more often on dry land than in the water).

What should I do? (Really, what should I do?).

Learn to inhale with your head rolled towards your least favoured direction . . . (That's easy for you to say. Why don't you try doing something you're not accustomed to – and don't forget to inhale from time to time).

At first this might seem difficult, but you must learn it in order to master the style. (No comment).

When you learn to breathe facing your least favoured side, the trick is getting the knack of the rhythm. Inhale after every three strokes, rolling your head from side to side. (I often shake my head from side to side and I usually manage to breathe in at the right time, so why isn't it getting easier for me?)

Such rhythmic breathing satisfies your body's oxygen requirements. This is how most professional swimmers swim. (I don't like professionals. They make me sick, winning all the time. Then they stand there satisfied with themselves, as if winning were the most important thing in the world).

Besides, breathing on alternating sides allows your body to work in symmetry. You build muscles and flexibility evenly on both sides of your body . . . (I don't care about flexibility. Symmetry is good, but right now I just need to get out of the water).

I'll make you remember me
or,
Usually the suffering only lasts a few days.

NO, I won't cry. Next time I won't sit there like a helpless victim and I won't accidentally knock over a flowerpot. When I see Alex, I'll go downstairs and ask him simply what he's doing tonight. That's the kind of question they ask in the movies and I think it's a pretty good one.

It wasn't a bad plan, just difficult to implement. I had to go to work almost every day, and even when I was at home, Not-Alex was usually there too. Allowing him into my life had been a big mistake. When you live at someone else's, you can always move out, but when someone's living at your place, there's nothing you can do.

Nobody had ever lived in my apartment, so I didn't know what to do. If there was a fly in my kitchen, I'd squash it. Some time before, I bought a dog, but after a few weeks, I got so tired of him that I walked him as far from home as possible, tied him up outside a shop and left him there. Neither solution would work for Not-Alex. Which was too bad. We both would have been better off.

I'd fantasize about coming home to peace and quiet. But I never did. After cleaning the house and putting supper on the table, Not-Alex was always there waiting for me. This annoyed me, and whenever I opened the door to Not-Alex's smiling face, I'd feel the urge to kick him.

Once Not-Alex really crossed the line. He bought a table, sawed its legs at an angle so that the table would be level, and set it up in the big room. That was really too much. I don't need things to be perfect or to have all my dreams come true. I kicked that table of his to pieces and threw it off the balcony.

A few minutes later, Alex's (and Not-Alex's) mother picked up all the pieces and took them inside. I have no idea why. Maybe she was building a canoe.

Not-Alex never asked what happened to the table.

That day, I lost my cigarettes twice, scalded my hand and burned a hole in my dress. Don't imagine that I threw the dress away. The hole didn't bother me. The dress was mine. I could do with it whatever I liked.

It was too bad that Not-Alex's suitcase wasn't mine; I would have done what I liked with it as well. All I could do was look inside. There was nothing interesting in there. The contents hadn't changed. And the box; it was lying in the suitcase as if it had never been taken out. I took it out and placed it inside my armoire. I thought I might still need it.

As soon as I saw Alex, I would tell him I had his box. I wouldn't tell him where I got it. I thought he would be pleased. After all, it's nice to get back something you lost.

Alex was nowhere to be seen; he had disappeared without a trace. Greek always said that you can achieve anything as long as you're patient and persevering. He was right. Sooner or later, everything that falls into the water gets tossed out.

Time after time, time before time, from time to time

or,

Usually only lips speak.

TIME IS not continuous; it's fractured into separate moments. 99% of these moments are insignificant. We tell time based on the remaining 1%.

"What are you doing this evening?" Alex asked.

Yes, it was Alex who asked, not me. You don't believe me? I don't either. Did I say that it's easy to predict the future? Well, it is, more or less.

"I'll be at work," I lied. I didn't have work that day.

"Can you not give it a miss?"

I thought for a minute.

"Fine."

I wanted him to see how much I was willing to sacrifice myself for him.

"I have your box," I said, glancing down at the floor.

"What box?"

Why did he always pretend that he didn't understand me? I took the box out of the armoire (why do those bloody doors creak so much?) and passed it to Alex.

We were sitting on the couch in my room. The couch was tilted to one side and Alex was leaning towards me. He didn't seem to mind. It's lovely when you don't have to make excuses. Alex was relaxed; he had no intention of leaving.

I didn't know what to say. I never know what to say. Sometimes this frustrates me. I want to say something interesting, but nothing seems interesting enough. But I did remember one thing.

"Alex?" I checked to make sure he hadn't fallen asleep, as we hadn't spoken for a good ten minutes.

"Yes?"

"I was wondering about abstract painters. How do they come up with their ideas? What do they see in their work?"

"And how do they turn their concrete subjects into something abstract?" Alex finished for me.

"So you know?" I asked.

"No."

"Do you draw?"

"No, but I play an instrument," Alex said.

"Not the French horn I hope?"

"No. The flute."

"Where do you play the flute?" I asked.

"In the mountains, for the sheep." He laughed.

Normally I smoked inside, but Alex wasn't smoking, so I went out onto the balcony. Alex followed.

"The yard looks peculiar from your balcony." Alex leaned through the railings to look down. "I've lived in this house all my life and have never been to the second floor."

"Who lived here before me?"

"Bloody hell, look at all that rubbish!" Alex was astounded. "If you want to catch someone's attention, you could drop a flower pot on them."

"I did once," I admitted, but immediately wished I could take back my words.

"And?" Alex was interested. He was so tall that his head skimmed the roof of the balcony.

"Nothing. He didn't even notice," I said. "So who lived here before me?"

"An old man. I think he was my mother's lover," Alex said, his voice laced with loathing.

"Why didn't you like him?"

"He was always playing the harmonica."

"Is that why you didn't like him?"

"No, not because of that. He played well."

For a moment Alex said nothing more. I lit another cigarette.

"I saw a movie once about accordion players somewhere in South America. The only thing they did was to compete with each other to determine who was the better player. The protagonist was dying. The film depicted his journey to find the accordion maker who'd made his accordion many years before. He wanted to return it to its creator."

"And?" Alex prompted. "And?" was his favourite question.

"He found the accordion maker, but he'd been dead for many years. He was mummified and lying in state in the village square. His daughter dusted him every few days."

"So what did he do with the accordion?"

"I don't remember. The accordion had horns."

"Horns?" Alex said.

"Yes. Cow horns." I said. "Tell me again about that man who lived here before me."

Alex was silent. We went inside without saying a word and Alex shut the door to the balcony.

I stood staring out of the window. Alex walked over and stood behind me. He put his arms around me. I stroked his hands. We stood there in an embrace. It was peaceful. He was much taller than I – my head only reached his shoulders. He touched my face, my lips. I closed my eyes.

I couldn't move because he gripped me with one arm while caressing me with the other. The position he was standing in made it impossible for me to touch him. But he could do whatever he liked with me.

He wanted time to stop; he wanted that the moment to be a marker between what happened before and what happened after. He succeeded.

We made love in silence. He covered my eyes with his hand, probably so that I couldn't see who he was. I stroked his shoulders. I liked the disproportionately large muscles at the side of his neck. Although he was naked, it didn't feel disgusting to touch him.

Normally, Alex was abrupt and irritable, always on the offensive, but making love, he calmed down, became less restless; he was pleasantly still and slow, no longer angry with the world or himself. He felt no need to rule the world; he became a nonentity, and was content. He kept his lips pressed against mine the whole time. At first this made it hard to breathe, but I learned to breathe differently. Although he didn't say a word, I could guess what he was going to do next from his lips.

He was strong and held me tightly, but the minute I moved, he would ease his grip on me. I felt as if he was listening to everything I had to say, even though I didn't say a word.

New names for things
or,
Usually things pass from one hand to another.

"ALEX?"

"What?"

"Tell me about the man who lived here before me."

"I don't know anything about him." Alex said.

"You don't know anything, but you didn't like him." I turned onto my side. "Tell me what you know."

"I think that these things are his. The furniture too. That photo on the wall was also his." I wanted to get up and take a look, but it was light out and I didn't want Alex to see me naked. I was afraid he wouldn't like what he saw; my legs are crooked, my stomach protrudes, and my bottom is nothing to write home about. In other words, it was better stay put, to lie there quietly.

"And?" I asked. I knew that I was making it obvious that I loved him. If you love someone, you start to imitate them. I wanted to ask if he had noticed, but he was saying something and I didn't want to interrupt.

"When I was little, he often sat out on the balcony. He smoked a foul-smelling pipe. His hair was long and wiry; my mother would often say that someday he would set his hair on fire and our house along with it."

"But he didn't?"

"No. But my brother and I were always afraid of him."

"Afraid?"

"Yes. I don't know why. He never came down. I never saw him anywhere else, only on the balcony. He never went anywhere. I have no idea how he lugged so much stuff up here."

"Did anyone ever visit him?"

"No. At least not that I saw. I can't imagine what he ate, or what he did during the day."

"Was he sad?" I thought that I would have liked this man. He didn't go anywhere; he didn't stick his nose into anyone's business. He lived quietly, not expecting anything from anyone.

"No, quite the contrary. He was always laughing at something, alone and out loud. Like a witch. I think he was a witch, except that he was a man of course." Alex had begun to enjoy talking about him.

"He always wore striped clothes. I don't know where he got them from. Sometimes he'd talk to himself."

"What would he say?" I asked.

Alex seemed suddenly frightened and melancholy.

"Nothing."

"He'd talk to himself, but he wouldn't say anything?" I tried to pin him down.

"He'd say that all children should be hunted down like frogs and roasted on a spit. Or better yet, they should be hung by their ears on the clothes line; their tongues should be cut out, so they couldn't scream. Their mothers should be sent to the nether world or at least locked inside armoires so they wouldn't bother him. Their houses should be burned down, but their ashes were not to be buried in the ground to make sure nothing would sprout from them."

Alex had begun to talk excitedly.

"He also said that he'd never die, because he'd been sent into this world to improve it. Then he would light his pipe again, which, after his outburst would smell even more foul. He sat and smoked as if it was nothing."

What an interesting man, I thought. I liked his ideas, only he didn't succeed in realizing any of them.

"Did he die?" I asked.

"I don't know," Alex said. One morning he wasn't on the balcony any more. A couple of years later my mother rented out his apartment to you.

I knew then that I would demand that Not-Alex move out that night. It was too hard being good. Someone else could have him.

Thanks to a lucky combination of atoms
or,
Usually it's easy to predict what will happen the next day.

THE NEXT day Not-Alex and I sat eating.

There are only two rooms in my apartment; mine and the big room. I chose the smaller room for myself. I don't need a lot of room. Not-Alex was always moving from one room to the other.

I liked my room. It seemed older than the big room. The furniture seemed older too. I liked the great big old armoire the best. Sometimes I would get inside and sit for a while. It was cool inside; it smelled of toxins and forest. The insides of the armoire were lined with wallpaper the colour of black wine, printed with silver ornamentation. (I wallpapered it myself, but it's better not to know this. I liked to think that it had always been there). The armoire doors were old, with a large mirror on the outside; they creaked.

The old man's photograph hung on my wall as well. I often looked at it. But he wasn't anything special. He was a man like any other. I didn't know who to be grateful to; I was so happy in the apartment.

There was nothing else in my room, only that armoire, the photograph and a large, white shag carpet. The wooden walls were old and dark and the windows were small. My room was always dark. And so what? Who says that light is better than dark?

I had to go to the larger room quite often because Not-Alex's suitcase was there. Besides, I had to pass through it to get outside or onto the balcony.

I never allowed Not-Alex onto the balcony. He had no business creeping around there.

My apartment had no kitchen. The estate agent who had leased it, said that it was one of the big draw-backs about the place, but I didn't see anything negative about it. There's plenty of food that doesn't require any preparation, so why did I need a kitchen?

We were eating in the larger room.

"Not-Alex, who lived in this apartment before me?" I asked, my mouth full.

"My father lived here. He was much older than my mother. He disappeared for a while. When he returned, mum wouldn't let him back into the apartment, so she gave him the attic. Although she refused to admit it, I would see her come up here quite often, but she never let us come up. When my father died, mum stopped talking. I don't know why. I suppose she only liked talking to him." Not-Alex chewed calmly as he told his story.

I wanted to ask if Alex knew about this, but when I was with Not-Alex I never mentioned Alex; we pretended he didn't exist.

It was late and I wanted to sleep and so once again I failed to demand that Not-Alex move out. Tomorrow. Everything is better tomorrow.

Naked, completely naked
or,
Usually the same is never the same, just very similar.

THE NEXT day. I was with Alex, eating. It was exactly the same spot I had eaten with Not-Alex the day before. We were eating the same food (to be more precise, it was the leftovers from the day before). The only difference was that the day before it had been in the evening, while with Alex it was in the morning.

I realized I'd never seen Alex in the evening or at night. I wondered what he looked like in the dark.

"Sometimes everything seems so meaningless I can't get out of bed," I said.

"What about other times?" Alex asked.

"It's the same." I laughed.

Alex spilled food on himself. He would always get food on himself when he was eating. He took off his shirt and sat in front of me completely naked. I have no idea what came over him, why suddenly he trusted me like that.

"Alex, you look like the man in the photograph." I didn't want to ask him about his father directly, but I wanted to somehow initiate the discussion.

"Everybody resembles each other," Alex said, with food in his mouth.

I don't know if he really didn't understand what I was trying to say or if he was just pretending. I wanted to ask if he would come again the next day, but I was afraid of ruining everything.

"Have you ever had a dog?" I asked, because it seemed to me that in the background of the photograph, next to the armoire, there was a dog. (I couldn't tell if it was the same armoire or not).

"Yes, I have. I still have one."

"Why haven't I ever seen it?"

"Because he's invisible."

I could quite believe it, because even in the photograph the dog was barely visible.

"Alex, do you ever have nightmares?" I asked wanting to know everything about him.

"Have you heard me scream at night?" Alex laughed.

"I'm serious," I said.

"I do," Alex said a little more seriously. "I dream that I'm alone on the balcony, I'm smoking that stinking pipe and I say that all children ought to be hunted down like frogs and roasted on a spit. Or better yet, that they should be hung by their ears on a clothes line and their tongues cut out so they cannot scream. Their mothers should be sent to the nether world, or at least locked up inside an armoire, so they wouldn't get in my way. Their houses ought to be burned down, but their ashes shouldn't be buried to make sure nothing sprouts from them."

Alex, it seemed, was able to repeat everything he said word for word. That wasn't easy.

Alex and Not-Alex looked alike. Only their eyes were different. Alex's eyes were closer together, more to the front of his face; like a predator with eyes in the front of its head so that it can better see its prey. Not-Alex's eyes were far apart, at the edges of this face, like a herbivore, the better to see the predator sneaking up from behind. I don't know if their characters were determined by their eyes or vice versa.

I went to my room to look at the eyes of the man in the photo. They were exactly like Alex's. I was sure that their mother's eyes would have been like Not-Alex's, those of the preyed upon.

When I went back into the big room, Alex was reading a book. As I entered the room, he picked up an orange and hurled it at me. Obviously I wasn't able to catch it and the orange smashed against the wall.

"Reflex training," said Alex.

"You're mad!" I was angry.

"No, I'm not. But the orange is." Alex stood up and went to clean up the remains of the orange.

I imagined that he would throw it out, but instead he picked it up and rubbed the juices in my face. You ask why I didn't defend myself? He attacked me unexpectedly, and besides, he was much stronger. (I really don't want to know that that's how everyone justifies themselves.) When I came to my senses, I was soaked. I looked ugly and the juices stung my skin.

Without saying a word, I went to the bathroom. I locked myself in and ran the bath. Before getting in the tub, it occurred to me that there was no reason to lock the door, so I unlocked it, undressed and got into the bath.

When Alex opened the door, I turned on the strongest shower setting and aimed it at him. He wasn't in the least bit surprised. It seemed like he had come into the bathroom in order to be sprayed. Besides, he was naked. He was expecting me to get even; there was nothing unpredictable about what I did. Anyone in that situation would have acted the same way.

Alex sat on the floor leaning against the bathtub. I stroked his hair. I liked the fact that Alex didn't get into the bath. Not-Alex would have. That was it. It was the last day. I was going to order him to move out. It might be awkward, and perhaps I would never find out if he was going to take Alex's box, but I would think of something.

"Alex, don't you think that the most perfect way of meeting someone would be to get hit by their car, or to hit them with your car? Just like in the movies."

He was silent. He turned, looked at me and smiled. That was enough for me. The whole time I sat stroking his hair, getting it wet, messing it up and then combing it straight with my fingers. I liked his hair. It was so pleasantly straw-like. Not-Alex's hair was completely different; unpleasantly straw-like. I don't know why that was.

"It takes only five or six combinations before a person's genetic makeup completely dissipates and then the person is completely gone," Alex said.

I didn't understand how this was related to what I'd been talking about, but I nodded. I didn't even know what I was agreeing with. I agreed, that was all.

I think a person is most vulnerable when they discuss their fear of ceasing to exist.

Every time I was with Alex it was the same. It didn't matter if we were at home, if we were making love, or just talking. Every time was wonderful. A miracle.

Natural obstacles
or,
Usually there's no need to answer the question.

A FLY has a unique biological autopilot and can overcome obstacles even while asleep.

EVEN WHEN I'm awake, I'm always bumping into something.

Why did I have to choose that street? I should have sensed I'd run into Anastasia.

"How lovely! This is my first time here. I don't know why I've never been here before, it's so romantic."

Anastasia leapt into my arms and kissed me on both cheeks.

I took a look around. I didn't see anything romantic. I was angry at myself. So what if it was Anastasia's first time, I still should have anticipated it.

Anastasia was in an ebullient mood.

"Look! I bought a fur hat. I came here to buy food for the fish. There was an ad in the paper, so I came, but I couldn't find the store. But it doesn't matter. I found this instead." And again she shoved the fur bundle in my face.

I wanted to tell her that her hat was probably made from a dead badger because that's what it looked like. When Anastasia put the hat on, I was expecting, for some reason, badger droppings to fall from it if she shook her head too hard.

Of course nothing fell from the beaver. I was imagining things as usual.

We sat down in a run-down café for some coffee.

"Is it possible for the Almighty to create a rock so heavy that he can't lift it himself?" Anastasia asked.

I looked around, unsure if the question was directed at me.

"What?" I was baffled.

"The Almighty. Can He create a rock so heavy he can't lift it himself?" Anastasia repeated.

How would I know? I knew that it been a mistake to run into her. She was sat by me like some kind of Chimera, an invisible snake's tail tucked beneath her, a badger cap instead of the head of a lion. I would have been better off having a smoke.

Anastasia was undoubtedly my best friend. After all, I should have a girlfriend; everyone has one. Anastasia was my only friend, therefore my best friend. When I thought about it that way, even the hat was no longer so hideous. And the surroundings really were romantic. The wind picked up plastic bags and other bits of rubbish, while at the next table four girls were getting into a heated argument; they were probably best friends too.

Following that logic my friend Anastasia's friend Greek was also my friend (my friend's friend is also my friend).

And my enemy Not-Alex's enemy, Alex, was also therefore my friend (my enemy's enemy is my friend).

My friend Anastasia's enemy – me – was also my enemy (my friend's enemy is my enemy).

My enemy Not-Alex's friend – me – by this logic was also my enemy (my enemy's friend is my enemy).

All loose ends tie up beautifully. There are no logical exceptions. The Arabs were right. I checked it for myself and can prove it.

The shouting of the four best friends grew louder. Real friends behave like that all the time. But Anastasia and I found it a little uncomfortable. They yelled so loudly that we found it impossible to hold a conversation. We moved to the next table. Immediately the waiter stuck his head out from the door thinking we were running away without paying the bill. He was no mind reader. Even though I liked the idea of running away, and Anastasia in her cap looked suspicious, we were in no hurry to leave because we had nowhere to go.

Anastasia's hat was too big; it kept slipping over her eyes as she drank her coffee.

"Don't you want a hat like this?" Anastasia asked.

I wasn't sure why I should want something just because she had it. What would I do with the hat if Anastasia gave it to me? I'd leave it at *France*. Greek could put it in the box where he puts whatever customers have left behind them.

But Anastasia had no opportunity to gift me the hat as something astonishing happened. A wounded bird crashed onto our table. It was large and bloodied, unimaginably horrible. I'd never seen a wild bird so close. Anastasia jumped, spilling her coffee on the bird. The bird seemed dead, except that its wing and claws twitched randomly. The waiter stood calmly in the doorway pretending nothing had happened.

I sat motionless. There was no point jumping up, shrieking. The four friends were still shouting at each other. Only Anastasia and I saw the bird, it seemed. I was convinced her hat was to blame for everything that happened.

Time stopped, like in a photograph. Then suddenly, as if it understood its picture had been taken, the bird flapped its wings and took off. No trace of blood remained on the table – only the spilled coffee. Anastasia sat down and fixed her hat. The waiter came back to life as well. He tidied up the table, and asked if he should bring Anastasia another cup of coffee to replace the one she'd spilled.

We pretended nothing had happened. A group of young men sat down at the next table, one of them very attractive. They invited us to join them. I would have, but Anastasia wouldn't move. I stayed by her side.

"Why is their coffee so bland?" Anastasia asked apathetically.

How would I know? I said nothing, which didn't seem to bother Anastasia in the least.

The easiest way to predict the future 3
or,
Usually you can't return to the same Antarctic twice.

THE ANTARCTIC has its own area code: +627.

IT DOESN'T matter, what you expect; the future will not be as you imagined.

Even in the Antarctic.

What can we do if we're not happy about it?

Not all people look alike
or,
Usually, if the body is beautiful, then the soul is beautiful. But a beautiful soul does not guarantee a beautiful body.

ANASTASIA DIDN'T tell anyone about the bird. I don't know why. I never saw her hat again either. You can't blame Anastasia; everyone wants to be happy and they don't want to take any responsibility.

Everyone wants to be beautiful too. Not everyone can be beautiful, but it doesn't matter because in the end everyone is unhappy.

When I ordered Not-Alex to move out, he too was unhappy and beautiful.

The truest words

or,

Usually we lie every other sentence. But the remaining sentences are truthful.

GREEK STARTED to take kerning classes and seemed much happier. I've no idea what he was doing there; I think he was learning how to use herbs and spices. Which would be handy for a bar owner.

"Oh, come on now." As usual, Anastasia disagreed. "Kerning is the adjustment of spaces between letters. If the adjustment is done well, then the spaces between letters are uniform or at least very similar."

I wondered why Greek needed to go on this course. Would it help with the writing of his novel?

He attended the class almost daily, except for Wednesdays and Sundays, so he came in to *France* less often. Without him there, we were free to do what we wanted.

There were others that worked at *France*, not just me. My favourite person there was Peter Illinois. I'm not sure which was his surname and which was his given name; we simply called him Illinois.

Illinois was tall and thin and spoke with a voice so deep that the first time you heard it you glanced around, wondering if someone behind him was speaking. But there would be nobody there, except perhaps his shadow. Illinois had long, thick, black hair, which we sometimes convinced him to let down. We would caress his hair, because it was so shiny and beautiful and would tell him that his hair was shiny and beautiful and Illinois would smile and tell us he'd seen better. But we hadn't, so everything we said to him was the truth. Scout's honour.

Illinois was attractive; thin, but muscular, with an aquiline nose and multiple earrings in his nose and ears. He was a good person; he said we could come to him for help if ever we needed it. And besides that, Illinois was the only person who hadn't worked at the old *France*. That was his best attribute.

"Blanca, invite me to your house some time," Illinois would say.

"No," I would answer.

I wanted to tell him that there was only one person I would ever invite to my house, but I didn't. One time, however, I did. Why hide it? From then on, Illinois began to try to guess who that person could be. (He's still guessing).

Illinois loved birds. At home he had two birds; a raven and a roller to be exact. He brought us photos. I couldn't tell which was which, but then I don't know anything about birds and I don't care.

"You could ask Illinois what kind of bird it was that day," I suggested to Anastasia.

She turned as pale as a ghost; turned, in fact, as pale as she had when the bird had crashed onto our table. I didn't say another word about it. From then on, Anastasia avoided Illinois; she practically stopped coming to *France* on the days he was working.

"There's something suspicious about him," Anastasia said. "He must have made up that name and surname. Have you ever heard such a name?"

What a stupid old woman, I thought unkindly about my friend. She's the liar, but she accuses others of the same thing. And what's more, Greek and Not-Alex called her Ana. I don't know if they didn't know her real name, or if they were just trying to ingratiate themselves with her.

I mention Illinois only because one day, when I had the day off, Alex brought the box in to *France*, gave it to Illinois and asked him to pass it on to me. I had just walked into work when Illinois told me that he had a present for me. I had no idea why he would want to give me a gift.

Illinois teased me, saying he would give me the present only if I told him who I wanted to invite to my house.

"Marie Curie," I said, so he'd leave me alone.

"I'm sorry to disappoint you, but she's dead." Illinois laughed.

There was nothing funny about that; I knew.

"Bill Gates."

"Did your computer break down?" Illinois laughed and laughed. He was always laughing, which was nice.

"What difference is it to you?" I refused to give in.

"Tell me or I won't give you the box."

"What?" I asked. Did he really say "box" or was I hearing things?

"I won't say another word until you tell me who you want to invite." Illinois continued to taunt me.

It was fun. Illinois was so light. Lighter than anyone I'd ever met.

"Fine. I'll tell you." I agreed.

"I'm waiting."

He was waiting. *France* was full of people and everyone wanted to make their order. That was, of course, why they came, to order what they wanted. When it had opened, everyone at *France* had preferred to sit by the window, so they could look outside; now they all wanted to face in the other direction to see the painting of Greek's woman. I liked that. Not everyone wants to look at immobile things.

I read somewhere about a certain type of torture: they capture a poor wretch, tie him to a chair and turn him to face a white wall. Completely white, without any marks or scuffs. Not even any shadows. And the poor wretch goes mad. People can't look at nothing for long. I don't understand why they don't try imagining something. I also read, however, that they use the same treatment for psychiatric patients. As they stare at the white wall, they gradually grow calm and are cured. I guess the same medicine works differently for different patients.

"Tell me," Illinois would remind me every time he walked by.

Either he was very young, or he just looked that way.

I came up with many names: a striptease artist; all the world's presidents that I could think of; the grizzly bear and its cub from the Berlin Zoo; Greek; the Dalai Lama; the man who had brought the box; Madonna, and many others. But Illinois wouldn't believe me. He'd simply laugh and laugh.

One evening, when we were about to close up, Illinois said that if I wasn't going to tell him, then I would have to invite him to my apartment.

I agreed and he gave me the box. I don't know why he called it a gift.

The easiest

or,

Usually, the things we do most often are the least significant.

THAT WAS the easiest day of my life. I convinced Illinois to meet me in town rather than at my apartment; it was obvious he would agree, though he pretended he wouldn't for a long while. I knew he was teasing me; that's why it was so easy.

We went out on a rowing boat. He kept rocking the boat, pretending he would tip us over but I knew he wouldn't. I was calm and rocked and sang to myself. I don't remember what song.

We stopped at the library. Illinois chose his books slowly. It was interesting to watch how he would first brush his hand across the front cover; if something didn't please him then he'd put the book back. If it felt good, he would keep looking. He chose his books like others choose their beds; first he would check to see if they were stylish and comfortable.

"You won't find anything that way," I said.

"So what?" Illinois laughed.

He didn't find anything. We left the library empty handed, just as we had arrived. Having nothing to do, we went for a stroll. Illinois was wearing black leather trousers and a grey, plain T-shirt. He never wore anything with a logo on it. I was wearing a pretty, but uncomfortable, tight, green dress. I don't know why I had dressed so stupidly.

"Your dress is missing something," Illinois laughed.

"I thought it had too much," I disagreed.

"It's too long."

"Way too long."

In the nearest shop we bought a pair of scissors and Illinois cut my dress just above the knee. His first attempt didn't come out very evenly. In my reflection in the window of the shop we passed I could see that one side of the dress was longer than the other. We had already tossed away the scissors – why carry them around? So we went back to the same shop and bought another pair. Illinois trimmed the longer side. It was much better then.

"There's still something wrong with it." Illinois was not appeased.

He dragged me to another shop and bought two handfuls of metallic flowers. One by one he glued one of the handfuls to my dress and the other to his trousers.

We didn't have anything to do, but this didn't bother us in the least. We strolled around town and were happy. It was nice to be with Illinois. He didn't expect anything from me or from anyone else.

We had to go back to his apartment then, because it was time to feed his birds. Each bird had its own cage, but their doors were kept open, so they could come and go as they wished.

"Aren't you afraid they won't come back?" I asked.

"No." Illinois laughed. "If they don't return, they don't return. They're wild after all; they only come back if they know they don't have to."

Throughout the whole day Illinois didn't touch me once. To be more exact, he never came closer than half a meter. That's why that was the easiest day of my life. I didn't have to consent. I didn't have to say anything, or explain anything, or feel guilty, or happy. I didn't have to do anything at all.

We listened to music, some unusual songs of a northern tribe, which to this day lives deep in the taiga. I couldn't tell if they were singing words or just making strange sounds.

"Why do you need to understand everything?" Illinois laughed.

They say a dog resembles his master. I don't know about dogs, but I'm sure that a bed resembles the person who sleeps in it. Grumpy people sleep on creaking beds, while romantics choose waterbeds. Illinois's bed was long and narrow and hard. I tried to lie down on it and was surprised to find it comfortable.

"Don't you roll over in your sleep?" I asked. The mattress was abnormally narrow.

Illinois laughed.

"Sure, I do. I rise up into the air, roll over and then lower myself back down."

I had seen on TV that some people can do this. How convenient, I thought, because a bed like this would be good enough for them.

Illinois had a balcony. Balconies are also like their owners. Illinois' balcony was narrow and long and, most importantly, empty – there was not a single thing on it.

"Where did you put everything?" I asked, surprised.

"What do you mean 'everything'?" Illinois didn't understand.

"Everything that was on the balcony."

"There wasn't anything here."

What a strange balcony, I thought. I'd never seen one like it.

When we went out walking again we ran into Polina. I noticed her from a distance. She was more beautiful than ever. I couldn't stop looking at her. She came up and hugged and kissed Illinois. They chatted a bit. Only then did Polina notice me. She hugged and kissed me too.

"I'm going to meet my mother," Polina said and left.

"Oh goodness!" I was surprised.

"Why do you say that?" Illinois asked.

"Do you know who her mother is?"

"No."

"Anastasia."

"Oh dear!" It was Illinois, now, who was surprised.

"You see what I mean!"

"They're not at all alike." Illinois laughed.

"Not really. But who knows? They might look alike if they stood next to each other."

This has happened several times to me before. Things seem unrelated, but if they occur one right after the other, or if you put them together in your mind, you realize they have something in common. They share a mood, a style, or something else. For example, Greek and his woman. At first nobody could see what they had in common, but after a few months, people began to comment. "They're like two peas in a pod. Their lips, their noses, even their fingers are identical." Everyone began to suspect that Greek had given the painter his own photograph to paint, not his woman's. The painter had only to add longer hair, breasts and the olive tree. But I didn't think that; I never suspect anyone without good reason.

During our walk we met forty-six of Illinois' friends. Each hugged and kissed him, not that that meant anything. Others needed him, so I began to need him too. I couldn't help it. I always need what others have. I, too, wanted to hug and kiss him. His kiss would be so easy.

Sweet confusion, sweet experiments
or,
Usually the desire to change remains a desire.

"YOU NASTY cow!" Anastasia accosted me the moment I walked through the door of *France*.

She shoved me as she passed by. Fortunately I struck the bar, otherwise I would have fallen. My entire body throbbed.

Every morning Anastasia stopped by *France* to get a coffee. That morning she'd found a feather in her coffee; a brown feather, several centimeters long. I don't know why she thought I was responsible.

"She's so horrible," Illinois said about my friend and laughed. "Let me take a look, did you hurt yourself badly?"

A black and blue mark had started to form on my back. Illinois brought me some ice, wrapped it in a tablecloth and pressed it against my back.

"Tell me when you can't stand it anymore."

What? I wanted to ask, the cold or you? I could see that Illinois was falling in love with me. Let him love me, I thought. No harm in that. He wasn't as annoying as Not-Alex.

Greek announced that Not-Alex had moved in with Anastasia. He didn't seem pleased about this, as he kept repeating, "I hope it's only temporary."

That day we went to buy Illinois some new earrings. Once a year he changed all his old earrings for new ones. What an interesting person, I thought.

I had no doubt that it was Illinois who had put the feather in Anastasia's coffee.

Across the sky

or,

Usually, the more people you meet, the emptier the world seems.

WHAT IF I were a feather, a two-centimeter-long brown feather?

I would soar across the sky.

A bird would find me, carry me to its nest, place its eggs on top of me and hatch baby chicks. Then it would throw two of them out because there wouldn't be enough worms, not enough for all four chicks. And I would witness it all.

The next year, the birds wouldn't return to that nest. In a few years it would rot and I would drift to the ground. The wind would lift me up and I would soar across the sky.

I would drop onto the pavement in the city and stick to an old woman's shoe. She would take me home and we would be all alone there, me and my lady. When she died, her shoes would be thrown out along with her other things, and me. I would witness it all.

Then I'd soar across the sky.

Illinois would put me into Anastasia's coffee. Anastasia wouldn't notice and she'd swallow me. And I would witness it all. Or Anastasia would notice, call me a nasty cow, and shove me. I would hurt my back. And I would witness it all.

I would fall into Illinois's hair and he'd take me home. He would notice me and hang me on one of his earrings. But I would come unglued and fly across the sky.

The rain would flatten me to the ground. Wild boars and pigs would trample me and bury me. But children would find me and fasten me to their arrows. They'd play with me until they poked their eyes out and I would witness it all.

I would fall onto Alex's box. Gently he would blow me off, leave the room and shut the door. I would fly out the closed window and soar across the sky.

And from above I would see a crushed snail, probably the very same one. And I wouldn't feel any pity.

I'd fall into the water. Face first. I would be warm and frightened. I wouldn't be able to breathe. When you train yourself to stop breathing, you cause your cells to work more efficiently and you live longer. I need a long life because I'm a feather.

A fish would swallow me and that fish would be swallowed by another fish. But I would pass through undigested, just as I was. Feathers are not digestible. I would swim across all the oceans, soaking up water until the oceans were all dry and then I'd soar across the sky.

I would descend on the portrait of Greek's woman. I'd wipe away her tears.

I would stick to Red Dress's eyelashes and see the world through her eyes. I would see two happy children, for whose welfare she earned her living as a prostitute. She isn't bothered by this. I'd see how she moaned, lying under any man no matter what he was like; heaving in pleasure, even for the most disgusting client. I'd see how each time her vagina was wet, her thighs ready for anything. How she would ask to have her hands tied, because if she could touch him as well, she wouldn't be able to bear the pleasure. I'd see her upper lip quiver and a bead of sweat form, which she would lick dry immediately. As she closed her eyes, she would clench me tightly. And now both of us would moan with pleasure. Men wouldn't understand where the second voice was coming from, but they wouldn't have time to think about it, because the woman's body would suck everything from them. Clients would keep returning to her; they would pay her big money, to feel that huge heaving body, that unearthly moaning and to experience those few seconds one more time. Afterwards, the woman's body wouldn't let go of them right away, the muscles of her vagina would continue to squeeze them tightly.

When Red Dress would let me go, again I would soar across the sky.

I would land, finally, on a windowsill at *France*. I would burn it to the ground and destroy myself. Nobody would notice, not even me.

I would soar across the sky. Everything would disappear, except for me, because the sky would be mine. And the sky would never end. Only then would I be able to cry as much as I wanted.

Moustache
or,
Usually moustaches don't suit everyone.

SOMEBODY PAINTED a thick, black moustache on Greek's woman. It wasn't me. The woman in the painting resembled Greek even more now.

Of course Greek was angry with us. Who else could he blame? He took it back to the artist the same day to get the moustache removed. I thought this was a waste of time as the moustache was quite becoming. But I was afraid to tell Greek.

Without the painting, *France* looked empty. Fewer customers came. We were all in mourning; we felt the loss of the woman. We all waited for her to be brought back.

Anastasia no longer drank coffee alone every morning; she had Polina. They would come in, sit down and drink coffee without saying a word. And what's wrong with that? Why must people talk when everything is clear? Nobody, not even Illinois for whom everything was easy, dared to go up and ask, "Anything else, ladies?" It was obvious they didn't need anything else.

I watched Polina. I couldn't not look at her. I didn't feel guilty. After all, she let me look.

Illinois brought me flowers every morning, I don't know why. It wasn't right away that I noticed he had also started to grow a moustache. But, unlike Greek's woman, the moustache didn't suit Illinois. I didn't say anything, however.

On Illinois's birthday we closed *France* in the middle of the day and went out to buy him a present. It didn't take us long because I knew what to get him. At the first shop we went to, I bought him a thick silver chain. It wasn't exactly what I wanted, but what was important was that it was light. The chain suited Illinois very well. It accented his body's leanness and flexibility. From that day on, I never saw Illinois without the chain.

"That was quick," Illinois said. "We still have some time."

"Time for what?" I didn't understand.

"Greek won't be back until the evening. When we get back we'll have a couple of hours to open *France* so that he wouldn't even notice we were gone."

After lunch, *France* was always half empty. It was no great loss that we closed it. We locked in the customers who usually sat in *France* from morning until night.

"What if they want to go out?" I asked.

"They never have before, so they won't now. Let them sit a while." Illinois laughed.

I never had any problems with him. Depending on the day, life was either easy or very easy.

We sat in the park and counted crows. Illinois told me about how tsunamis are formed, about how cyanide is made, and how to restore old frescoes. He told me how the Franciscan order was founded, how moveable bridges are built, how the spleen functions, how chocolate with chilli peppers is made, how cave-dwellers traverse caves, how to make chewing gum at home, why the atomic bomb explodes, how to grow a bonsai tree from an ordinary tree seed, how organs work, how Modigliani died, how to tell a female crow from a male crow and how to break a safe's code.

Illinois talked a lot, which was mesmerizing. I wanted to remember every second of his conversation. After our conversations, I would wonder what he was thinking about, but when we met, I would always forget to ask. Not because I was afraid. I would simply forget.

Illinois was the first man I didn't move in with. I don't know why. But it did make me realise why I'd burned down the old *France*; so that there would be a new one and Illinois would come.

One door is the entrance,
the other is the exit
or,
Usually when you need a dish, you can't
find one. It's the same with everything.

LIQUIDS, WATER for example, do not have a shape like other bodies; that's why they are able to flow and take the shape of the container you pour them into. The molecules of a liquid combine into groups. They flow because the parts do not combine rigidly, and thus they have greater freedom to move.

I'M SORRY, but I really could not have given birth to that child. If you cannot do something, then you shouldn't have to.

It had been an eternity since I had seen Alex. Well, actually four months and three days. He had disappeared. And if I had met him, I'm not sure what I would say. It seems to me that if you can't say something, then you don't need to.

I was liquid. I spilled because there was no plate, there were no edges to hold me, that's why I poured out and nobody was able to collect me.

Gifts

or,

Usually people like to receive presents.

ILLINOIS AND I didn't have anything to do during the day, so we decided to give everyone gifts. Just like that, for no particular occasion. It's nice, I think, to give gifts.

We wanted to give Anastasia a feather and to get an adhesive moustache for Greek. However, this time we didn't think it would be funny. But a gift doesn't have to be funny, does it?

Illinois gave me a box, almost exactly like Alex's. I threw it out immediately. I couldn't even look at it. I had one already, I didn't need a second.

I bought Illinois a stuffed crow. He can rest easy: this crow wouldn't fly away. The next day I found a nearly identical stuffed crow in the rubbish bin near *France*. But that didn't mean anything.

I take pride in choosing the right gift. You can give someone a person. Obviously, only if you've got somebody spare. And there are always spares; you just have to look around. My mother, for example, gave me as a gift to my sister. My sister could do whatever she wanted with me; my mother didn't care one bit. Later, my mother gave my father away to her friend. After having given everybody away, she was able to relax and live her life lavishly, alone. Guess what my mother says when I talk about this? You guessed it. "You're mad."

Or, you can give an animal as a gift. People love getting animals. For example, a man once gave me a bat. That was a wonderful gift; unfortunately it flew away. And I gave my friend a rooster. A real rooster with a red comb. I think roosters are beautiful birds. My friend loved the gift but after a while, the rooster disappeared. I didn't ask what she had done with it. It's not polite to ask. Give a gift and forget about it.

I heard that some people give stars. But I wouldn't want one.

I still haven't talked about gifts of fate, but I think people appreciate those gifts the least. By the time they figure out it was a gift, it's usually too late.

For three days, Illinois and I tried to figure out what to give Greek and Anastasia, but we couldn't think of anything. Oh well. They wouldn't get gifts.

When I turned five, one of my aunts gave me a rocking horse. That same night, I knocked out its teeth. I didn't like the expression on its face; its teeth were too large. With the teeth gone, the horse became my favourite toy. A week later, I tore off the supports it rocked on. I had seen real horses, and knew that they stood on four legs, not on springs. I turned my horse into an ordinary horse; without the rocking it was easier to imagine I was riding it. Only I couldn't sit on it anymore; its legs were uneven and unable to support a standing horse. So I broke off its legs. I didn't need them. I still have the remaining part of the horse; why would I throw it out? As I said, it was my favourite toy.

I told the story to Illinois.

"I think you did the right thing," he said.

I thought so too.

"I'm glad you liked the horse's head." As usual Illinois was laughing. "If you'd sawed off his head as well, it would have been hard to know what the thing was in the first place."

That time I think Illinois was right.

You shouldn't punish someone twice for the same offence

or,

Usually making new friends is easy.

I HAD put the box on top of the armoire in my room and was guarding it carefully. It was my greatest treasure, but I couldn't be too happy about it because the box didn't belong to me. I thought long and hard about how to get it back to Alex.

I hadn't seen Alex for half a year (six months and seventeen days, to be precise). Illinois said that if someone or something disappears, it's because they want to. What nonsense. Illinois was too young to understand anything. What about things? Do they disappear when they want to? Of course not. How do you explain robberies and kidnappings? But when I said this, Illinois laughed.

I decided that giving the box to Alex's (and Not-Alex's) mother was probably the most reliable thing to do. If she had given the box to her son once, she was sure to do so again.

I climbed down the ladder and knocked on her door.

"I've been waiting for you for a long time," Alex's mother said the minute she opened the door and saw me.

It was the first time I had heard her speak. Even when renting the apartment, she had never spoken to me herself; she always sent an agent.

We went inside and Alex's mother led me to her room. What I saw astounded me. I had always expected Alex's mother's apartment to be as full of rubbish as my balcony, but it was the opposite. The room we stood in was bare and it was identical to my own room.

The walls were wooden, old and dark, the windows small. It didn't look like the room ever saw the light of day. Alex's mother didn't seem to care about light either. Only people without any other problems worry about such trifles.

I knew that her apartment also had a large room, like mine did; you couldn't get into the small room without passing through the larger room. So great was my shock that I hadn't noticed what it was like. (I determined to look the next time I visited). The only thing I could recall was that there was no table.

Like me, she lived in the smaller room. She apparently didn't need much.

Adjacent to one wall there was a big armoire with a large mirror on the outside door. The door was ajar. Through the crack I could see that the inside was lined with wallpaper the colour of black wine decorated with silver patterns. Perhaps I had sleepwalked and wallpapered her armoire as well as mine? There was no other furniture in the room, only the armoire and a large white shag carpet, just like the one in my room, only much dirtier.

On the wall was a photograph of an old man exactly like the one in my apartment. Alex's mother must have looked at it often because it was faded.

I couldn't tell where she slept, because I didn't see a bed. Friends who visited my apartment couldn't tell where I slept either. I think you should keep your bed hidden, because a bed says a lot about the person who sleeps in it. It's important to reveal as little about yourself as possible.

"We wanted to feel like we lived together," Alex's mother said.

It took me a few moments to understand she was talking about the old man in the photograph and herself. Why were there only photos of him? Where were her photos?

"At first I had my photos up as well, but I didn't like them, so I took them down," Alex's mother said. This time I wasn't surprised; I had quickly realized she could read minds.

I had no reason not to believe her. Women often don't like their own photographs. Besides, women prefer to do things the way they want.

I wanted to ask why they didn't live together if they wanted to. I didn't have time to open my mouth, when she spoke.

"I never talked. I would sit quietly. That's why he attacked me with an axe. After he returned, I ordered him to move out, because even then I had no intention of talking."

So what had made her so talkative with me? Was she afraid I would attack her with an axe? She shouldn't have worried.

I knew her name was Pandora, but I didn't dare address her that way. I don't think you should address an older person by their first name unless they invite you to, so I waited (to no avail) holding the box on my lap. Alex's mother paid no attention to the box. She didn't have the slightest interest in why I had come to visit.

"Do you have a twin sister?" she asked. "Sometimes a woman visits you; she looks a lot like you, but she's not you."

"No, I don't, though I agree that sometimes someone who looks a lot like me but who isn't me comes to my apartment," I answered.

"Ah."

We drank coffee flavored with cardamom. She never left the house, but bought herself things like this, I thought.

"Would you mind giving this box to Alex?" I asked.

"To Alex? Really?" She asked.

"Really." I confirmed. Who else?

"Fine."

"She took the box and placed it on the armoire. It was clear that she was going to guard it with care, as I had.

"You have no balcony," I said.

"No," she agreed, sadly.

"I think it's important to have a balcony," I said.

"Very."

We were both silent for a good half hour. It wasn't at all uncomfortable. Time passes quickly.

"All my life I've treated people like dogs," Alex's mother said.

I wasn't shocked. Many people behave that way.

"They've never forgiven me," she continued.

People always come up with reasons for not forgiving someone, or for criticizing them.

"I grew so tired of them that I locked myself up in this apartment and now I have no contact with anyone," Alex's mother said after a few minutes.

Maybe it was for the best, I thought. She seemed happy. I liked her. I decided that she would be my friend. Perhaps an even better friend than Anastasia.

Alex's mother took a radio from the armoire and we listened to some music. A man played the violin and a woman sang. The songs seemed old and sad.

"It sounds like it's you singing." I don't know why this idea came to me; the voice wasn't the least bit similar to hers.

"It is me," Alex's mother said, to my great surprise. She began then to accompany the woman on the radio. The violinist played for both of them.

When Alex's mother started singing, her voice changed completely, it became thin and raspy. She changed too. She held her head and arms higher, even her hair seemed to rise up on her head, and become fluffier. I didn't like these changes. I wanted the old Alex's mother back. I was relieved when the song ended and the radio ended up back in the armoire.

"You won't forget to give the box to Alex?" I asked.

"To Alex?" she asked.

"Yes, to Alex," I confirmed.

"Fine. Next time I see him," she said. I didn't ask when that would be. What difference did it make, as long as she gave it to him?

As I studied her from up close, I could see that Alex's mother wasn't old; she only pretended to be, perhaps so that everyone would leave her alone. After all, nobody wants to be around old people.

"Before I had the twins, I had a girl," Alex's mother said, after a long pause.

"What happened to her?" I asked.

"She went to live with her father. Her father was a violin-ist. We toured together. I sang and he played. When I moved in with the twins' father, he wouldn't let me take the girl. So she stayed with her father."

I thought I would like to have been that girl. But that couldn't be; I had my own mother. I hadn't seen her in a long time and if I were to see her, she would say, "You're mad." Yes, I am mad, but that wasn't my fault. I would rather have had a mother like the woman sat in front of me scratching her head.

"That's a beautiful ring," I said. The ring was beautiful, with a huge ruby held in place by the tentacles of an octo-pus. Or perhaps it wasn't an octopus. Perhaps it just looked like one from a distance.

"I won't give it to you," Alex's mother said sharply.

"That's all right," I said. "You don't have to give me everything."

There was a large hardback book on the rug. I thought it might be a cookbook, full of recipes. When Alex's mother turned around, I bent down to take a look. It was a beauti-fully illustrated guide to face painting. Quickly, I returned to my seat. I didn't want her to think that I was snooping. It's not nice to snoop around your friend's house.

"Do you want something to eat?" Alex's mother asked, remembering that she was a mother, even though she wasn't mine.

"Yes."

Children visiting their parents should always want some-thing to eat, even if the parent is not their own.

Alex's mother heated up some pasta. It wasn't very tasty, but that made no difference to me; I ate it. I figured that when you're visiting parents, even if they're not your own, if you ask for something to eat, you should eat it, even if it doesn't taste nice.

"My hair's not natural. I'm wearing a wig," Alex's mother said.

"Oh," I said.

I finished up the pasta, thanked her, and went home. I had spent a good half day visiting her.

A week later, I found the box on my doorstep. "He wouldn't take it," was written in chalk on my door.

Greek changes women. And time.

or,

Usually people don't want to give, or
they don't have anything to give.

FINALLY THE workmen brought Greek's woman back.

"Listen, something's not right," Illinois whispered in my ear.

"With what?" I asked, confused.

"With Greek's woman."

"What's not right?"

"She's not the same; she doesn't look herself anymore,"
Illinois noted.

"You don't remember what she looked like before the
moustache," I said.

"I remember. I'm telling you, she doesn't look like herself."

"Who does she look like?"

"Anastasia," said Illinois, surprised.

"Oh, come off it." I wasn't convinced.

"Take a look."

Illinois cradled my head in his hands, turned it to the
painting and held it there for a few moments. There was no
doubt; the new portrait was of Anastasia. Nothing else had
changed; the same clothes, the same olive tree, just a different face. I wasn't sure if that was what Greek had wanted, or
if it was a coincidence. I was afraid to ask.

"Ask Anastasia. She's your friend after all," Illinois teased.

"Sure. I'll ask her as soon as she comes in," I said.

I didn't feel as comfortable with Anastasia as I pretended. I didn't dare to ask her right away, only some thirty minutes later. Of course Illinois made a big show, gesturing repeatedly for me to ask her.

"Anastasia, we think it's you in that portrait," I said as nonchalantly as possible, but loudly, so that everyone in *France* would hear (Greek wasn't there).

Anastasia didn't deign to look at the painting or at me.

"Leave me alone so I can drink my coffee," she demanded.

What more could I do?

Illinois and I stood behind the bar observing Anastasia secretly. I knew she wouldn't be able to bear it and eventually she would have to take a peek at the painting. And so it happened. She turned her head slightly, but, surprised by what she'd seen, forgot to appear disinterested and gawked at the painting. She stood up and went closer. Everyone in the café put down their coffees to watch.

Anastasia turned to me and asked for a knife. Not knowing what to do, I looked at Illinois; he laughed and motioned for to me to give her a knife as quickly as possible. I did.

Anastasia walked towards the painting and stepped on a chair so that she was eye-to-eye with the woman. She raised the knife and scraped off the remaining evidence of a moustache on the woman's upper lip. Then, she got down from the chair and returned to her seat and drank her coffee as if nothing had happened.

Anastasia seemed sad. She didn't have anything to give to Greek.

Three little pigs
or,
Usually our heroes grow old alongside us. Polina sat down at the bar to talk to Illinois.

I DON'T think it was her intention to torment me. She was talking to him, that was all. Every time I passed by, I listened in on their conversation, but I didn't hear anything suspicious.

"Illinois?"

Polina pronounced his name in such a way that all Illinois could say was, "At your service, Princess."

He actually said that. I wanted to tell him she was no more a princess than I was. But it's probably better not to meddle.

There were lots of customers and I had to run around taking everyone's orders. I tried to keep Illinois and Polina within earshot. Polina leant towards Illinois slightly, her top button unbuttoned. I didn't say anything. I do the same thing sometimes.

Even though he was on the opposite side of the bar, Illinois would take Polina's hand every once in a while. I didn't understand why.

Polina was telling him that she had been to the mountains and that it had been beautiful. So what? Everyone finds the mountains beautiful. What was there to tell? Illinois said the only way he would go sliding down a mountain would be on his bum; he was afraid enough to go down a hill, never mind to drive or ski down a mountain.

Polina said she knew. I wondered how.

Every time I passed them, they were talking about books. It was possible they were talking about a completely different topic, but changed the subject whenever I passed by. There was nothing I could do about it; I couldn't prove anything.

All books were about eccentrics, Polina told Illinois, they are about people incapable of living in the real world; that's why their prototypes cannot exist.

Illinois said that he had read plenty of books about the most ordinary, everyday human lives.

Polina wouldn't agree. She claimed she had never read such a book.

It took me a while to notice that although Polina disagreed with everything Illinois said, she mimicked all of his gestures. When he raised his arm, she did too. When he leaned to one side, or opened his eyes wide, or gave a big yawn, she did the same. I don't think she was doing it on purpose.

How nice it is for Illinois, I thought, working at the bar; he could spend his entire shift talking to people as long as they were seated close enough. And believe me, Polina was close enough. Too close. I wanted to tell her it wasn't polite to practically lie on the bar, but I didn't want to call attention to myself. Better to listen some more to what they were talking about.

Few people know, said Polina, that the three little pigs are not three separate characters, but three aspects of the same character. It's always the same character building the house, not a different one each time. But each time, he learns from his mistakes. Thus he's continually evolving. Even the wolf is not a distinct character, but another metamorphosis of the same character. The pigs are not threatened by an external being, but by another "I", the sad and doubting part of the same self. That self kicks and it puffs, trying to knock down everything that the constantly evolving little pigs are slowly and patiently building. Only when the pigs reach the state which enables them to chase the wolf away would they conquer doubt and feelings of guilt; only then could the story end.

If that's true, I thought, then you are the princess and the pea, sleeping beauty, the nasty stepmother and the prince who kisses sleeping beauty. You are the ugly duckling, and everyone who refuses to accept him into their flock. You are the pied piper of Hamelin and the children he seals off in a cave with a boulder for revenge. You are the twelve brothers turned into crows and the sister who rescues them. I don't know. Perhaps.

Illinois quietly cleaned the bar. He didn't laugh. The whole half day that Polina had been at the bar, he didn't look in my direction once.

Do your own thing and don't
worry about the consequences
or,
Usually life is easier when you pretend
to be something you're not.

*MIMICRY: THE phenomenon by which an organism takes
on the colour and form of an inanimate object or an organism
of another species in order to increase its own chances of survival.*

*Some bacteria and micro-organisms are capable of mimick-
ing the molecules of macro-organisms. That's why the immune
system of a given person or bacteria recognizes them as its own
and does not initiate a response to the infection.*

*Some plants have adapted mimicry for reproductive purposes.
Their flowers resemble certain female insects and they dissemi-
nate a similar scent, which attracts males.*

AND LET him. Let him not look at me. Let him talk to
Polina or whoever he wants. I don't need him. I have Alex.
So what if eight months and twenty-six days have passed
since I last saw him? We don't have to see each other every
day. He disappeared, but I know that he still loves me and
will return some day. After all, sometimes people have to
leave suddenly and they have no way of getting in touch to
let you know where they are. All kinds of things happen. But

sooner or later they do come back. It's rare for someone to disappear for good. I just have to wait. And so I waited.

As it's better to keep busy while you wait, I thought that perhaps I should go to talk to Alex's mother again. She was my friend now, and you can stop by your friend's house whenever you want.

You can stop by, but that doesn't mean that they'll invite you in. I knocked a few times on her door, but she wouldn't open it. I tried in the morning, the evening and during the day. I knew she was home. One time I saw the curtains move, but nobody opened the door.

I thought of setting fire to the door, then she would have had no choice. She would come out right away. But I decided to wait.

One evening, when I returned home from work, someone in the yard called me.

"Hey. Hey!"

I turned. Alex's mother waved to me from the narrow crack in her door. I wanted to pretend I hadn't seen her and climb back up my ladder as if nothing were the matter, but she called me again.

"Hey. Hey!"

I didn't have a choice. She called so loudly, that I couldn't pretend not to hear. We went inside her apartment. Alex's mother made some coffee and placed some biscuits on top of a pile of books.

"They're made with thyme blossom; have some!" she offered.

"Eat them yourself," I wanted to say, but I didn't. She had ignored me every time I knocked, but now she was pretending to be my friend.

"He wouldn't take the box," Alex's mother said.

"So what else is new?" I wanted to say, but I didn't.

But I did ask, "Did you have something you wanted to tell me, or can I go now?"

Alex's mother pretended not to hear. "Sit," she muttered and sat down heavily next to me. Like a yogi, she curled her legs beneath her. She's just a lonely, middle-aged woman, I thought, and besides that, she's my friend. I should be more understanding.

I thought that she was like the fairy tale of the wolf and the seven little goats. She was the mother who went out on an errand, leaving her children at home alone. She didn't know where she was going or why; there was plenty of grass right next to their house. Even when she had locked her children inside and gone off, she felt that she was not rid of them; they hadn't disappeared. She and her children were one and the same. But she was also the wolf who came and devoured the children and in doing so she devoured a good part of herself. Of course the children opened the door to her; it's harder to fool children. They saw that it was their mother not a stranger.

She regretted how she had behaved and was afraid that she had allowed the wolf to rage too much; she didn't control herself and destroyed a big part of herself in the process. She knew that the wolf had to be punished, because that was the nature of conflict; you destroy your opponent or he'll destroy you – there's no other option. Her story ended when the wolf, a stomach full of stones, which she put there, drowned in the river bed. She, the goat and the little goats, lived happily ever after.

*   *   *

I realized I had no reason to be there. I didn't have the box with me. I wouldn't be able to ask her to give it to Alex a second time. I didn't dare ask where Alex was. It's not polite to force yourself onto someone who doesn't want you; besides, I didn't want to drag her into what was already a complicated story.

I was conflicted; I was tired and wanted to sleep and I knew that Alex's mother wouldn't say a word about him. She would pretend he didn't exist and wordlessly would try to convince me, as if her thoughts, which she didn't believe herself, could fly through the air flapping their wings like a flock of invisible dragonflies and settle in my head. Things don't happen like that, unfortunately. There's no such thing as invisible dragonflies.

I didn't expect to learn anything about Alex. In that apartment sitting next to that woman I felt as if he were sitting somewhere close by, in the armoire, for example and was breathing against my face. Unconsciously, I brushed my hand through the air. Alex seemed so real that with every breath I felt I was inhaling a part of him. I breathed in as deeply as possible and exhaled as little as I could, until my head started to spin and I had to start breathing normally again.

"If you nod off and your book starts to slip out of your hands," Alex's mother said, "It's better to let go, because if you don't, you'll tear the binding in half. And what good is that? A torn book is of no use to anyone, not even to you, because nobody wants torn things."

"Yes, it's important to let go at the right moment," I agreed.

"Do you understand what I'm telling you?" she asked.

"Yes," I said, "and I detest you for saying it."

"Well, that's a pity." Alex's mother sighed.

She was like a fly. A fly's leg is a kind of 'chemical eye'; the little hairs on the sole of its foot act as a chemical lab. With just one touch, the fly can determine the material a thing is made of. Alex's mother's chemical laboratory was even better. She didn't even have to touch anything. At a metre's distance she knew exactly what was what.

She even looked like a fly, sitting there sprawled out, with her invisible wings tucked beneath her, pretending she didn't see anything with those huge, expressionless eyes of hers. But just try to move your hand a little closer and you would see that she was alive and had been watching you. She saw more than you did yourself. The whole time she had been prepared to defend herself, to fly off and then descend again in a lethargic state in order to observe you even better. It was a rude way to behave, I think.

We spoke for a long time. She told me her about her life. The story was odd because she made no mention of her husband or of her children, as if they had never existed.

Every sentence in her story began with the word "I". I thought that was beautiful. If you want to tell a story, talk about yourself, not other people.

I learned that many years before she had studied medicine, but after a few years, she had realized it was a loathsome profession and dropped out. All her life she had dreamed of becoming an architect, but she had never achieved her goal. Whenever she saw a new face, she said, in her mind she imagined it as a building. Faces are inspiring, she said, because nowhere else can you see such strange shapes or more deformed details. In her mind people stopped being people and were transformed into houses built on chicken legs.

I interrupted her story and told her that I thought that this was a great idea. She asked me not to comment on her story but to just sit and listen. I said I couldn't promise that.

I learned that she had never held a steady job; she made her living doing odd jobs. She spoke a few languages, so she often earned money as a translator. She enjoyed translating song lyrics most and lectures about extraterrestrial beings landing on our planet. (Unfortunately she had only came across two such texts.)

As a translator, she had many adventures, but she only told me about one. There was an important city council meeting. The mayor, a man with a huge head, a wide face and ears that stood straight up, was hosting an important foreign delegation. His face inspired Alex's mother to imagine an imposing cathedral like the Notre Dame in Paris. The head of the delegation, a bishop who was a tall, thin man with a long, expressionless face and wearing a cassock was trying to convince the city government to build a small church in the central square (Alex's mother drew in his place a wooden country outhouse with a rhombus-shaped hole in the door). The city was large, he said and there weren't enough churches for all those who wished to worship. Alex's mother liked the priest and although she was not a believer, she agreed with his idea of building another house of prayer in the city; it would be a good place to shelter from the rain, or people could use its main entrance as a meeting place.

Unfortunately the mayor held firmly to his position that more than anything the city lacked public toilets, and this, in his opinion, was a more important basic need. Since space was at a premium, one had to choose what was more essential.

It was an interesting story, I agreed, but Alex's mother again asked me to stop commenting – to just sit and listen.

She also told me she had graduated from music school and was a talented percussionist, although she had always wanted to sing. Unfortunately her father had decided that drums were a better pastime for a girl like her.

"What kind of girl?" I wanted to ask, but Alex's mother said that if I didn't keep quiet, she would stop with her story, so I didn't say another word.

Alex's mother coughed nervously and wiped her hand through her dirty, artificial hair. I drank coffee with cardamom, and, from time to time, spat out the grounds. A bee buzzed around the room. Alex's mother stood up in the middle of our conversation and swatted it with a flyswatter. The bee fell to the ground, where it lay writhing in pain. Alex's mother picked it up and crushed it between her fingers. Wiping her fingers on her yellow skirt, she took out a Gallois and sat back down next to me.

After smoking the cigarette, she continued with her story. Having listened to all her stories, I understood that nothing worth telling had ever happened in Alex's mother's life. Her stories were a convoluted hotchpotch of trivialities. Either that or she had no idea how to tell them.

If it hadn't been for the scent of Alex in the air, I would have gone home long before. I barely listened to what she had to say. I tried to imagine what Alex did when he was in that room; what he ate, how he sat, how he breathed in his sleep, how he spoke, how often he blinked. After all, when you love someone, every detail is important.

Every time Alex's mother noticed my attention wandering, she'd say, "You're not listening anymore!"

I would say that I was. What else could I say?

That night, Alex's mother disappeared. I never saw her again.

Later, someone told me that after I had left her combing her artificial hair that very morning, Alex's mother had fallen from the highest bridge in the city and died.

I don't know if the autopsy founds rocks in her stomach. I wasn't sad because I knew that only the wolf had died; the goat and her kids were still living peacefully somewhere.

It wouldn't have surprised me to find that she had wanted to walk along the railing. I also wouldn't have been surprised if she, like I, could have swum ashore had she not fallen in too close to the embankment where the water was too shallow.

It's safest to take the middle path
or,
Usually while some play, others cry.

GRADUALLY ILLINOIS had become the soul of *France*. He was attractive, calm and perpetually happy. Greek wasn't happy, but he had no choice but to get used to it.

Illinois understood his value. He let his hair down. He played with us. It's important to play. People develop during play.

Greek muttered that it wasn't allowed, that he would shed his hair everywhere, but his hair was nowhere to be found and anyone who did find a hair was happy. Greek had to put up with it because Illinois's hair attracted people to *France*. He even began talking about moving the stock cupboard to the basement and renovating the vacated space to make another dining room.

"My little deer, bring me this, that, and the other," Illinois would say to me. He always called me his 'little deer'. It was lovely, because until then I'd been called goat (by Greek), nerd (by my mother), orangutan (by my classmates), scum (Anastasia), mouse (Polina), sunshine (Not-Alex), moon (Alex), Medusa (some other man), plucked chicken (my sister), rose (Red Dress), mandala (Alex and Not-Alex's mother).

I liked 'mandala' the best – you're like an ornament built by other people, Alex's mother said. People tried and tried; they poured the sand beautifully, but never managed to clearly delineate the detail. But it's your own fault, she would say. You lack an inner attraction; you're unable to take care of yourself. The slightest breeze or the smallest wave knocks down what the others have put in place in you over years. And that's the end of it. It's as if all their work never took place. A big mess once again, Alex's mother used to say. That was our game: she instructed me and I refused to get angry.

"Listen, my little deer, what are we going to do today?" Illinois asked.

"Why don't we play hide and seek?" I suggested. "When someone comes to the bar, you go and hide! Or when they call for me, I'll hide behind a column."

"Or we can pretend that everyone who comes into *France* is French and we must speak to them in French," Illinois suggested.

"Do you speak French?" I asked.

"No." Illinois laughed.

Red Dress walked up to the bar and sat directly in front of Illinois. For the last month that had been her favourite place. She would sit there day in and day out, telling Illinois stories about her husbands. I'm not sure Illinois found this interesting, because although the men changed all her stories were the same. As she talked, Red Dress would play with a lock of her frizzy, white hair.

"What do you think? Does she have one red dress or many?" Illinois asked.

"How should I know?"

"We have to find out."

"I refuse to ruin her dress. Don't ask me to," I said.

"I'll do it," Illinois offered.

In less than a half an hour, Illinois had tipped over a candlestick pouring liquid wax on Red Dress. It was the first time I had ever seen her cry; I felt sorry for her, but there was nothing I could do. I was interested, though, to know what she would wear the next day. Unfortunately our experiment didn't work; the next day Red Dress came in wearing a red dress and it was impossible to tell if it was the same one, or new.

Illinois was keen to try again, but I forbade him from doing so. I was a good person, but Illinois took pleasure in bullying others. He did it easily, without the slightest sense of malice and with a smile on his face, as if it was a game.

"Listen, my little deer," Illinois said. He wouldn't leave me alone. "Kiss me right here in the middle of *France* and everything will be clear."

I was intrigued, what would be become clear? I liked clarity. And so I kissed him. Everyone had heard him ask but I can't say that they seemed terribly interested. Don't ask me if I enjoyed kissing him, because I don't know; I had the feeling that I was kissing a statue. The kiss didn't affect me in the least. It didn't evoke the slightest bit of passion. I kissed him and that was that. It was nothing, so nothing became clear.

"Listen, my little deer," Illinois continued. He came up to me put his arm around me and whispered softly into my ear.

"Everyone tells me you're in love with me."

"Who is 'everyone'? Do you mean Anastasia?"

"How did you know?"

"She's my best friend, so she should understand me better than anyone else," I said.

Illinois thought I was joking, but I wasn't. However she was wrong – but what's the big deal? Friends can be wrong.

"I love you," Illinois whispered in my ear, clutching me still.

And I believed him. People who whisper about love are usually lying; if they loved you so much, why not say it out loud? I've always been suspicious of people who try to convince you that they love you at the slightest provocation. Even if it's true, why talk about it?

Illinois made it clear he wasn't going to let me go. From that day on it was as if he had become unhinged. Every time he walked by, he would touch me. For a good part of the day he held me in his arms. Greek would tell us that if we couldn't let go of one another, then we should work as a team, like a pair of Siamese twins. (I had no trouble letting go; I wasn't so sure about Illinois.)

"Listen, my little deer," Illinois repeated. "It's because of you that I wear my hair down. I started working here at *France* because I saw you in the window." It's certainly possible that he could have seen me, *France's* windows are large. "I'll do anything you say." Many had promised this before, but whenever I'd ask for something, they couldn't deliver. "I'll always love you." I guess he was clairvoyant; he seemed to know what would happen in the future. "Let's take a trip around the world." I never understood what that meant; even if you were to choose a direction and make a loop around the world, think of how much you would miss. There would always be a hundred different routes you could take. There were too many possibilities to make it worth even trying. "Let's . . ."

"Stop posturing." I interrupted, tired of listening to him. To an extent, I understood him; he lived with crows, he had no-one to talk to.

"Listen, my little deer, don't you know anything?"

"No, I don't. And so what? There are lots of things I don't know."

"You know that you love Alex, right?" Anastasia yelled across *France*, hearing our conversation.

"I know. I know perfectly well."

"Do you know more than you want to know?" Anastasia probed.

"Probably," I said, unsure what to answer.

"Do you know who loves you?" Anastasia asked.

Of course I knew. Alex. Alex loved me. You might ask, how I knew? Do you always need proof? Why can't I simply believe, not waiting for someone to validate that belief? In my opinion I can and so I believe.

Nobody, Nobody's
or,
Usually you shouldn't put your trust in your present good fortune.

CAN ANYONE cry my tears? The tears of someone who has everything and lacks nothing? I couldn't.

I wouldn't say that sadness made it difficult for me to live. No. But it did make it difficult for me to move; I couldn't get out of bed, I couldn't walk, I couldn't eat, or sleep. But other than that, I was alive, so I couldn't complain. I'm not complaining. I just want to describe how things were.

That morning my mother called. My mother. I didn't answer the phone because I couldn't raise my arm. To be honest I wouldn't have answered any other day either. I never answer when she calls, because she always wants something and I don't like people like that.

I also don't like people who say "God bless you" when I sneeze. They don't even think before saying it. Their "God bless you" is nothing more than an automatic reaction, a reflex. How can you trust someone who doesn't think before they speak?

I was lying there and couldn't even turn my head. No big deal, you say, what did you need to turn your head for anyway? And perhaps you're right. But I couldn't even move my arm and that wasn't very convenient if I wanted to swat a fly.

I would be lying if I said that I couldn't move at all. I could, but I could only make certain kinds of movement. For example, I could cover my head with my blanket, but I couldn't remove the blanket. And I couldn't do anything about it. I knew that I just need to lie there for a few days and wait and my sadness would pass.

Where does sadness go after it passes? I think it hides behind the armoire. You might disagree.

I'm not sure I could think at all. I don't know if what was going on in my head could be called thinking. I knew that if I tried to write something, my handwriting would have changed; the letters would be tilted to the opposite side. But I don't know why.

Sometimes you simply need to submit. To admit that you are no longer, that life has done what it wanted with you. It's not easy, but you must try. I knew that I would be allowed to move again once I admitted my complete defeat.

I had everything I needed. I didn't need anything else. If someone were to give me more, I wouldn't have taken it. I wouldn't have traded places with anyone. I didn't want to live a better life. I say this without any hesitation.

I lay and stared at the moon, but it did not look at me; I saw that clearly.

I know that people are different. Some pretend not to notice their sadness. Others can't. I can't. I don't know if that's my weakness, or my strength.

If I tried to move, the floor creaked and then the whole world would witness my struggle and that's something I didn't want. I only had enough energy for myself.

I didn't know exactly what time it was, but I could tell that it was evening. Night would fall, but things wouldn't be better, or worse. Darkness is just background. What difference does colour make? I don't believe the theory that the colours around us affect our happiness. I've never seen any proof. Sadness doesn't know colour; it pays no attention to it.

I wondered if things would get better if I got up. I got up, though I'm not sure my body did. I think a part of it remained lying in bed, head covered. I paid no attention. Stepping out onto the balcony I looked around. I could hear someone walking downstairs. Alex's mother, I thought. They must have tricked me into believing she had died. People often lie.

Several men left her apartment and when they had left with two huge boxes, all the sounds below ceased. I went downstairs and tried her door. It was locked. I inserted my key and turned it. It worked perfectly.

The apartment was empty, but everything else was just as it had been. It wasn't clear what the men had been carrying in the boxes, because there was nothing missing. I looked around. I opened the armoire. I found a ring in the pocket of one of the coats; the ring with the octopus and the ruby. I took it; there was nothing wrong in that, because, after all, Alex's mother had promised to give it to me. I took down the photograph of the man intending to take it upstairs to hang next to the photo in my room. It would be lovely to have two identical photographs next to each other.

It was getting dark, but I didn't want to turn on the lights. I was afraid that I would see something I didn't want to see. I rummaged through her pockets but found nothing interesting, just some old sweets, a rosary (that I did not expect), some hairpins, a brooch, a second, different brooch, a couple of pieces of coloured glass, a metal bell, a few coins, a tube of lipstick, an airplane ticket stub, a box of condoms (one left of three), a marble elephant, an ad for silicone breast implants (cut out from a magazine), a plastic flower, a silver pendant – a mermaid attached to the letter P, the pit of a peach (or some such fruit), a magnifying glass with a handle. That was it. I checked carefully one more time, but there was nothing else. I stuck the items in my pockets. I would take them home and arrange them on the windowsill in my room.

Should I take Alex's box down and place it among her things? He was bound to come someday, find it and take it with him. But I didn't think it was safe. He might not notice the box and throw it out with the other things. Or someone else might take it. I didn't think I should take such ridiculous risks.

I took her portable stereo as well. Locking the door I went upstairs. I was glad I hadn't taken anything else; it would have been hard to carry it all in one trip. I had the key. If I wanted something else, I could go and get it (and I did – a few days later I went down again and took the cardamom, which I found stored in a ceramic box. I also took an iron and the cup I drank coffee from.)

You ask if I felt better after walking around. I don't even know how to answer that. As I arranged Alex's mother's things on the windowsill, a part of my body was still in bed with my head covered. I turned on the portable stereo and listened to her unpleasantly thin, screeching voice. It relaxed me a little.

If there's a type of bacteria that eats not only good things, but also waste, why couldn't it devour my sadness? Impossible? Maybe you're right.

I lay back down. The part of me that stayed in bed moved over unwillingly and let me in. It didn't have much choice, just as I didn't. I covered my head with the blanket.

Could someone cry my tears? I couldn't. My cheekbones are so pronounced my tears wouldn't flow down my cheeks; they dropped like a waterfall. Not that it was important. But it didn't look good.

Who will guard the guards?
or,
Usually if a person disappears, permanently or temporarily, someone comes along to take their place. It changes nothing.

RENEWABLE RESOURCES – substances that naturally renew themselves; they therefore never become depleted. The sun, the wind and water are examples of renewable resources.

TO ANASTASIA people and animals were also renewable resources.

That night Anastasia dreamed she was a wounded bird crashing onto everybody's table. Startled and disgusted, the customers spilled their coffee. That was how it was and Anastasia couldn't change anything.

Anastasia didn't like birds, those strange, feathered mice. When she was little, she had a pair of beautiful birds in a cage. Every once in a while the birds would lay eggs and a few weeks later, their cage would be teeming with tiny, red, tweeting, squirming chicks. Anastasia couldn't stand chicks. As soon as the little pink chunks of meat appeared, she would collect them and throw them down the toilet, and flush. She did this over and over again. It was impossible to know if the birds missed their little chicks, but Anastasia's parents certainly did, wondering each time how they could have disappeared so unexpectedly. Anastasia didn't breathe a word as if it were she, and not the little chicks, that had been flushed under water.

Sometimes Anastasia wondered where they went. Perhaps they were lying in a pile somewhere, tweeting and squirming, as if nothing were wrong. Or perhaps they'd become fish and were swimming around in the Atlantic. That would have been a shame because the ocean was a dangerous place with all kinds of predators and fishermen lurking. Anastasia didn't want anything bad to happen to the chicks.

The dream lasted a long time; it felt like three days to Anastasia. But when she woke up, she was in a great mood. Not-Alex was sleeping as soundly as a child. Nothing strange about that, thought Anastasia, he is a child.

Anastasia got up, drank some coffee, smoked a cigarette, took a shower, and put on her makeup. As usual she stopped at *France* on her way to work to have a coffee with Polina.

It was impossible to know where habits come from, thought Anastasia. It seemed that you did something once, completely by accident and then for no reason you found yourself doing it again and again. That was how it was with her coffees with Polina. Who knows how they met at *France* for the first time, but from then on it became an obsession. Neither one would miss the coffee date for any reason. Even when Anastasia was sick and missed work, she still got up in the morning and went to *France*.

Their not speaking to one another wasn't planned – it just happened. It was an unspoken rule that if either one uttered a word, that would be the end of it; sitting together at the same table would no longer be possible. So neither woman ever said a word.

Anastasia liked everything at *France*, especially Greek's woman. It's not clear how accurate the portrait was, but the woman in the painting looked perfect. This irritated Anastasia because it wasn't realistic. Anastasia was a lawyer; it was her job to seek the truth. So, one morning, she came in earlier than usual and while Greek was tinkering about in the kitchen, Anastasia drew a moustache on the woman's face. Now she looked more realistic and Anastasia felt a sense of peace. When Greek cleaned off the moustache, Anastasia gave up. She was tired of fighting for truth.

The only thing Anastasia couldn't stand was Blanca. What a bitch, Anastasia would think. Young women always got what they wanted, without any effort. That, in Anastasia's opinion, wasn't fair. It was an irreparable injustice. And irreparable injustice was what Anastasia hated most.

Young women reminded Anastasia of those little chicks; they were pink; they tweeted and squirmed in the same way; unfortunately they were too big to toss down the toilet and flush away.

That morning Anastasia got to *France* early. Greek always liked this; he thought Anastasia came to *France* to see him, and coming early was a clear indication of her love.

Greek made Anastasia a coffee; a much better coffee than that he made for others. After all, if someone loved you, you should return the favour.

"Last night I dreamed about fish," Greek said, trying to start a conversation. Sometimes Anastasia would talk to him and sometimes she wouldn't. Greek tried every morning, just in case.

"Did those fish of yours look like chicks?" Anastasia asked.

They didn't look like chicks in the least, Greek thought, but, wanting Anastasia to like him, he said, "Yes, I suppose they did."

"Were they tiny and pink, with unopened eyes, like little mice with bird legs?" Anastasia prompted.

Not in the least, thought Greek, but if I tell her that, she'll scowl and stop talking to me. So he simply agreed.

"Yes, precisely." After a moment he added, "Just as you describe."

"And where were the fish?"

"In the water."

"In the water?"

"Yes, the Atlantic or somewhere," Greek suggested, though in truth he couldn't remember if there was water or not.

Although Anastasia didn't love Greek, she took pleasure in the fact that he was dreaming about her life.

"And what did you dream?" Greek asked after a few moments. But Anastasia didn't answer.

As much as Greek tried, the bond had been broken. Anastasia never let him sit at her table. So Greek pottered around *France* and went out to run some errands. Anastasia remained inside; so that she wouldn't leave while he was gone, he locked the door from the outside.

A few minutes later, someone unlocked the doors to *France*. Anastasia thought it was Greek returning; he was always forgetting something. But it wasn't Greek. It was Illinois with a woman. At first Anastasia thought the woman was Blanca. Blanca was always sticking her nose where it didn't belong. But it wasn't Blanca; it was another long-haired girl Anastasia had never seen before. Anastasia sat quietly in her alcove behind the column, so neither Illinois nor the girl noticed her.

The girl immediately started undressing. Illinois stroked her hair and whispered something to her, so quietly Anastasia couldn't hear. When she was completely naked Illinois fondled her body. He didn't undress, undoing only his trousers. The girl was fine boned; Illinois lifted her easily and sat her on the table. She didn't even have time to lie down; Illinois was already inside her.

Anastasia saw everything clearly; how Illinois entered her and withdrew; how he caressed and bit her. Bites marked the girl's body, but she didn't appear to care in the least. She clutched Illinois tightly between her legs, gripping the edge of the table with her hands as if afraid to fall. She didn't have to worry, thought Anastasia. She saw how tightly Illinois was holding that body which writhed in pleasure. His fingers were white.

Anastasia's body went numb. She wanted more coffee, but was afraid to move. She didn't want what she was witnessing to end. I could sit here forever, thought Anastasia.

Occasionally Illinois withdrew his penis and pushed away from the girl; then she would groan and crawl towards him, her eyes still closed, as if begging him to enter her again. When he had done the same thing a few times, the girl let go of the table and wrapped her arms around Illinois, making it impossible for him move. Anastasia was annoyed because the girl blocked her view. She could no longer see Illinois' penis sliding in and out.

With nothing to look at, Anastasia examined the girl's body. It was ugly; it was much too thin, bony, her breasts small. Anastasia saw the vein in the girl's neck pulsating.

It was the first time Anastasia had seen a couple making love. Everything was much more beautiful than in the movies. Besides, at the movies, there was no smell; here the sweet scent of sex permeated *France*. Anastasia inhaled the scent. She wanted at least a part of what was happening to enter her and stay with her forever.

Anastasia tried not to look at the lovers' faces. Lovers' faces are grimaced, contorted, ugly. But these lovers' faces were different. The girl's face was impassive, it showed no emotion at all, as if everything she was feeling was happening to her body below and didn't touch her face. A tear fell from one of her closed eyes and was absorbed by her hair. Anastasia wondered if another tear had fallen from the other eye which she couldn't see. A pity.

How long this went on, Anastasia didn't know. Her body began to ache, a lock of hair tickled her face. She could no longer stand not moving. She turned to the side, drank some coffee and fixed her hair. She tried to move as quietly as possible, but there was no need; they paid her no attention.

Whenever the vein in the girl's neck started pulsating, Illinois stopped moving and *France* became excruciatingly quiet. On a couple of occasions the girl tried to sit up, but Illinois wouldn't let her. With one arm he would push her down again, gently pinning her against the table. Finally he left his arm on her chest and the girl grasped it with both her hands. A bead of sweat flowed down Illinois's arm and disappeared under the girl's fingers.

Illinois bent over and kissed the girl, as if being inside her wasn't enough. He needed more. He sucked her tongue with his lips so that she would be inside him as well. He was moving in such a rhythm that she entered him on the same beat that he entered her. Everything was just as Illinois wanted it, because the girl couldn't move. She could only breathe deeply and moan softly once in a while, as if to show that she approved of what he was doing and enjoyed it.

When Illinois straightened up, Anastasia got a look at his face. She liked what she saw; Illinois was smiling. He didn't moan. He moved quietly, watching the girl and smiling. Just as he was about to finish, he closed his eyes. Anastasia couldn't tell if the girl was finished or not.

The girl is too young to understand anything, thought Anastasia, arching her back, all pink like a baby mouse, whimpering as she holds the man with her bird-like legs. I would never do that and I would never look like that, thought Anastasia.

Illinois picked the girl up off the table, and held her for a long time. The girl began to shiver and Illinois let her dress. They stood in an embrace for a few minutes and then the girl left.

After a while, Greek returned; Blanca came in, and later Polina. The first customers started arriving. The ordinary routines of the day began at *France*.

You can't have a city without houses
or
Usually even the most repulsive person is attractive to someone.

I DON'T remember if I told you that I'm blind in one eye. Completely. When I was little, I fell off a swing, hit my head and one eye became foggy. I was so frightened that I never told anyone. And to this day few people know anything about it.

I wouldn't say that it bothers me. I'm just happy to be able to see.

I went to Alex's mother's apartment again. I knew I was behaving badly, but she was my friend and special rules apply to friends. Nothing had changed in the apartment, which was hardly unusual in an uninhabited apartment.

I looked through her books, but got bored quickly because I didn't find anything interesting. But everyone has secrets and Alex's mother was like anyone else, I thought. I decided to search some more. Greek always said you mustn't give up without a fight.

I was right; hidden inside a book set deep in the bookcase I found a few photographs. They had been taken about ten years before in the same room. The curtains were drawn. Alex's mother was completely naked. I don't want to speak badly of the deceased, but she was ugly. Her hips were too low and too wide for her long, lean body. Her arms were too veiny, her legs too short. I don't know what possessed her to be photographed in the nude.

In one photo, she was leaning against a wall. In another she was seated and in a third, most unflattering of all, she was lying down. Her body reminded me of a piece of plastic melted in the sun. She wasn't even trying to pose or look more beautiful than she was. She showed off her body as if she were being examined, as if she were forced to bare herself, as people are when they must take a shower.

On the reverse of the three photographs was the same inscription; "I love you." No signature. Alex's mother must have written it to herself. I do this too. I can't see why it's a problem. If nobody else writes what I want, I do it myself.

There was also an old letter written to Alex's mother. There was no way of knowing who wrote it because the bottom of the letter had been torn off. The letter stated that its author had moved to a new house. This wasn't surprising as there is no city without houses. He had also written that he would never do it again (I didn't know what); once had been enough. He asked her to forgive him if she could. He briefly wrote that he was expecting to make new friends, but he was not having much luck because everyone around him was a swine and a cheat just like anywhere else. For example, today, he wrote, he wanted to buy a new suit, but he didn't have enough money (which, by the way, he was running out of and it would be lovely if she could send him some). Nobody would agree to reduce their price and sell their suits cheaper. How can you believe in the goodness of humanity after something like that? He asked. At the end of the letter, he mentioned that despite some difficulties, he still loved her, even though he didn't want to see her. He told her not to be sad, that she shouldn't torture herself with memories of their remarkable past. She should fall in love with someone else and send him some more money.

I don't know how Alex's mother responded, but I would have written something short and sweet. "Go to hell." Too bad there was no return address.

I took the letter and photographs. So? She didn't need them anymore. I also took her wristwatch. Now I would have two. I would set one watch five minutes faster than the other. I like ambiguity when I feel insecure or confused.

I found Alex's wedding license. Immediately, I ripped it up and threw it into the waste bin.

I made myself some coffee with cardamom and sat down in the place I always sat when I talked with Alex's mother. Then I moved to her place. Not for any reason; I just wanted to see how she felt sitting there.

A key turned in the lock and Not-Alex entered. He was not in the least surprised to see me.

"What's up?" he asked as if I were here every day and we'd seen each other the day before.

"I'm having a coffee. You want some?"

He did, so I made him some.

"You want to see a film?" he asked, sitting down next to me.

"Here?"

"Mother has an old movie projector."

Not-Alex took a box out of the armoire (I don't know how I had never noticed it myself), took out a few parts from it, plugged them into each other, inserted the film, pressed a button, drew the curtains and sat down next to me again. After a few moments, static could be heard and a flickering silent film appeared on the wall. Music played in the background; a violin accompanied Not-Alex's mother singing.

We sat like that for what seemed an hour. We drank coffee, watched the people on the screen walk, kiss, and dance, but we didn't say a word. When the film ended, Not-Alex put everything back in the box and closed the armoire.

I told him I had to go, but Not-Alex asked me to stay.

I don't know why I agreed. I don't know why I made love to him. Perhaps because I hadn't done it for a long time and maybe because I wanted to remember what it felt like to make love to him, what it felt like making love in that apartment. Not-Alex knew how make me forget how ugly I was. His eyes were like trick mirrors. Looking into them, I saw my own reflection, but more beautiful, a better quality, more expensive, a better brand.

That was how I felt every time I was with him. I knew that it would continue. Maybe it was wrong, but I couldn't let go.

There's no home without smoke
or,
Usually a dog's pelt isn't worth much.

YOU KNOW what? I decided to be happy. What was wrong with that? Everyone has the right to be happy.

From then on, I decided I would spend five minutes every morning telling myself a story about how pleasantly I would spend the day. I would make a pledge to myself. I would set myself up for goodness and happiness. This attitude would make it impossible to be distracted from my goal. These morning talks with myself would be important moments in my life.

Happiness is, I think, like smoke. The more you blow on it, the more there is.

I was furious with myself for not being happy. But from that moment on, everything, my life at its core, would change. I had already stated, "I want to be happy"; in other words, I had started my journey, which would change my life in remarkable ways.

It was 4:00 am. I was sitting on the rug, my heart was beating furiously. I was bathed in a cold sweat and filled with an impending sense of doom. What could I do? That's when I decided to be happy. I chose it for myself. Every choice can be changed later, but if you refuse to make choices, nobody can help you.

I tried to remember when I had been happy. I could only remember one occasion; that moment when I fell off the bridge and floated in the water with my face down. For a long time I hadn't breathed.

There was another time I was happy, just not so intensely. I was dreaming of a celebration. There were many guests (everyone was happy, they were dressed to the nines), and dogs. Many dogs of many kinds – large and small, long-haired and practically hairless, dogs with tails and dogs without, purebred and feral. The dogs were running around among the guests as if they were guests of equal stature, but they didn't help themselves to anything on the tables. Somewhere, in the distance, bells began to ring. It must have been late because the bells kept ringing and ringing.

I don't know why, but in the dream this fact didn't bother me in the least. The toll of the bells transformed the behaviour of the dogs. Each dog grabbed a guest and started to devour them, their clothes, jewelry and even their mobile phone. The guests didn't protest. Those being eaten calmly surrendered to their fate. They didn't scream and they didn't try to escape. The remaining guests continued to celebrate as they had been celebrating; they didn't look around, or try to change anything. The violin trio played up-beat classical melodies, some of which were familiar to me. The violinists tried to harmonize with the bells; they managed to find a complimentary rhythm and mood. While the bells tolled, the dogs enjoyed their spoils. Afterwards, everything returned to normal, only there were fewer people. There was no sign of battle, no blood, no panic. Only here and there a scrap of cloth from a fancy suit, or a piece of jewelry.

After some time, the bells resumed and the dogs rushed off to devour some more guests. This happened over and over again. The celebration lasted a long time. I saw that my turn was finally coming. But the dogs didn't touch me. When no more guests remained, and the bells began tolling again, the dogs lay down in a circle around me. As far as the eye could see, they spread out like a large fur rug. I was enchanted by the silence and the sense of peace, happy as never before, with no desire to wake.

I can't explain why I was happy. That's something you can never explain. Happiness doesn't depend on external circumstances. Happiness lies within. All you have to do is make up your mind to really want it and you can achieve it. I would evaluate my life and decide what I needed to do to be happier. I was prepared to dig deep into myself to find the basis for my decisions. I had to learn to listen to my heart because that's the only way I would find the true path to my own happiness.

I would stop blaming myself and others for my unhappy life. I would be mistress of my own life, not the victim of my environment. I knew that I had made mistakes; I could learn from them. I would enjoy every instant and value the simplest things as if they were marvelous events. I would not wait for the future, but enjoy the now.

I would be happy and infect those around me with my happiness. I saw a commercial once in which everyone who smiled got chocolate. But I would smile just for the sake of it, without reward. I would forget sadness; happiness would become my eternal, my all-encompassing state of being.

You don't believe I can do this? You don't believe I can be successful? You will see. You will see me happy.

There's no smoke without a fire
or,
Usually even if the fire doesn't burn, it warms you up.

I FELT like dust beneath the rug. Nobody saw me. That's why they trampled over me without regret.

Oh, sorry; I forgot that I had decided to be happy, to light a new fire in my life. I just didn't have time; I had to work.

France was full of people as usual. Greek was angry. Because he felt so at home at *France* (I'm not sure, to tell the truth, if he lived there or if he had another home), he shouted as much as he wanted, with no regard for anyone else.

"Why do you come here? Tell me why you come here?" Greek yelled.

For a moment I thought he was addressing me, so I told him that I worked there.

"What?" Greek asked, turning to me.

"I work here."

"Would you please shut up when you're not being spoken to?" Greek ranted.

Of course I could. I could be quiet even when I was being spoken to.

Greek turned to Anastasia.

"So, tell me, why do you come here?" he asked.

You could answer that kind of a question in a variety of ways. You could say, "I want to. That's why." Or perhaps, "I can stop coming if you want." I was interested to hear what Anastasia would say.

"Because I've never been to the real France, so when I sit here for a while, I can tell everyone that I've been to France."

"That's why?" asked Greek.

"I think that's an honest enough answer." Anastasia defended herself.

"And me?" asked Greek.

"Why do you come? Because it's your job."

"Don't pretend you don't understand the question!" Greek screamed. "Aren't you in the least bit interested why I'm here?"

"Interest is subjective . . ."

"I asked whether you were interested why I'm here," Greek repeated slowly.

At that moment, fortunately, a thin woman with thick glasses and disheveled hair worn up in a bun, dropped a glass and broke it and the sound of shattering glass caused everyone to turn their heads. Briefly the conversation was forgotten. I think the woman broke the glass to rescue Anastasia.

Anastasia took full advantage of the chaos. A few seconds later when we turned back to her, she was gone. I was thinking she would go directly to the travel agent's and buy a ticket and fly to the real France. Really, why would you go to the café day in and day out just to sit imagining it was France?

I considered telling Greek that it was Anastasia who had burned down the old *France*. Perhaps then he would stop loving her. As far as I knew, fire helped to cleanse the mind.

"I'm a slave to my emotions," Greek said. He said it calmly, without a trace of sadness in his voice.

"Yes," I agreed. "Humankind has evolved to such a degree that everyone is free to do just what they desire."

Greek started to cry. People often do that. When you understand that you are living only for yourself, you begin to feel sorry for yourself.

Red Dress dried Greek's tears and patted his head, as if he had regressed and become her third child. Greek broke three matches unsuccessfully trying to light his cigarette. Red Dress took the cigarette from of his mouth, lit it, and placed it back between his lips. Greek smoked his cigarette successfully and cried some more.

Red Dress stood next to him, pressing his forehead against her gigantic, soft breasts. Greek held onto her (it's natural to grab hold of something when you're falling) and caressed her bottom.

"Let me tell you, I did everything I could to make her love me, but it wasn't enough for her. It would be enough for another woman, but not her."

"At least she could have shown some gratitude," Red Dress agreed.

"I feel like a speck of dust brushed beneath the rug. She walks all over me without seeing me and without any remorse."

I wanted to tell him that I felt that way too, but I don't think it's nice to empathize with other people's feelings and appropriate them for yourself so I said nothing. I wanted to be sensitive and caring, like Red Dress, accommodating, very feminine.

Greek wiped his tears on Red Dress's dress.

"I know I'm not attractive," cried Greek.

"I think you are." I refused to agree.

"Lydia, light me another cigarette," Greek said.

It was the first time I'd heard him call Red Dress by name. I wondered how he knew it.

"You must find me funny." Greek raised his head and looked at us.

Neither of us was laughing. This calmed Greek a little.

"I've never seen her anywhere but *France*. Does anyone know where she lives?"

Nobody knew.

"Illinois, find out her address," Greek requested.

Illinois pretended not to hear. I, too, felt that Greek was better off not knowing.

"Forget that suicidal bitch," Red Dress advised. "She knows how to ask everyone else 'Do you know who loves you? Do you?'" With each question, Red Dress turned her head to the left side of the room and then to the right, so that each side of the room would hear her. Although her neck was thick, she was quite nimble. "She doesn't even know who loves her."

"Lydia, has anyone ever made coffee for you?" Greek asked.

"I don't need anyone to make me coffee," Red Dress pretended to be offended, "I earn enough to buy my own coffee."

"I made it for her every morning." Greek wept and wept, possibly because he was drunk.

"That's why I'm telling you to forget that ungrateful, depressive, social incompetent," Red Dress said. "Look at her; she's frigid, infantile, snobbish and old, without any brains or heart."

Greek raised his head from her breasts, as if to convince himself it was really Red Dress who was speaking in that manner, so cruel, so sophisticated, despite the fact that she had always looked like a kind-hearted dimwit. Illinois stood behind the bar smiling. There were a lot of customers, but nobody ordered anything. They knew that we were trying to console Greek and they wanted to see how everything turned out.

"You don't know her," Polina interrupted.

"You!" Red Dress snarled in such a way that Polina's desire to pick a fight evaporated right there and then.

The whole time they had been speaking Greek continued to stroke Red Dress's bottom, back and forth, back and forth.

"I know how to get even with her." Greek had begun to come back to his senses. He might even have been sobering up. "If you keep a goldfish in the dark or in running water, it loses its colour. Let's throw it into the sewer. By the time it swims out on the other side, it will be completely colourless."

"Then that bitch will celebrate," I interjected.

"Anastasia will never find out who did it. Nobody will be able to tell her because a goldfish only has a three-second memory." Red Dress nodded her head.

So that was what we did (or, to be more precise, that's what Illinois did. He didn't want to, but Greek forced him). We threw the fish down the toilet and gave it a good flush. We thought that Greek would feel better, but we were mistaken.

"I'm not developing as a person. I'm rotting," Greek whined. "Like an acorn that has never sprouted and was never eaten by wild boars, like a star, which didn't burn up and expire, like an old sausage in the fridge, like a blocked up tear duct . . ."

Greek, we realized, was inconsolable. People stopped gawking; they began to eat and drink again and to place orders. The scene had become too drawn out, too slow, and too boring.

Illinois gestured to Red Dress; a secret signal. Red Dress knew how to decipher men's looks and understood.

Red Dress took Greek home. She would warm him up. She would light his fire. I agreed; that was comforting.

My audience boos me, but I applaud myself
or,
Usually lost things resurface and if they don't, something new comes along.

MATTER: ANY substance that exists in the universe; everything that is not empty space. But even in matter, such as hard rock, there is empty space. All matter is made up of atoms and other particles and between them is empty space.

I HAVE to admit that I am also matter.

Sometimes I imagine that those empty spaces inside me expand and contract. Sometimes they grow so large that there's nothing left – only empty space. Then I am in full harmony with my name.

It's frightening. It seems that I will remain this way for eternity – empty as a hole – and nobody will be able to fill me up again. But time passes and again life fills me up, like a river carrying dry grass, rubbish and dead fish into a secluded cove.

Everyone had told me to stop obsessing about Alex. He had been gone for eleven months and two days. Everyone said that he had disappeared for good, but I thought that they were jealous. A person can't disappear like grain inside a mouse's stomach, or like a sound after the radio has been turned off.

Granted, even when we were together we were like a binomial star: like two stars that look close together in the sky, but which, in fact, are far apart. But I believed that things would be different when he returned; everything would be better. Why shouldn't I believe that?

It was time to look for him. Perhaps he had been planning to return for a long time, but didn't dare. It's important to fight for your love. I wrote a missing person's ad, stating that Alex had disappeared. I described him briefly and attached his photograph. It was only when I had made a hundred copies that I noticed I had left out a letter – instead of "Alex" I had written "Alx". It was a stupid mistake, but easily rectified. I redid the ad, made another hundred copies and posted them all over town. I asked Illinois to help, but he refused. A fair-weather friend, I thought.

Everybody had stopped speaking to me, though I could see them eyeing me with disapproval. I couldn't understand why. What was the problem? People often wrote ads like that for lost dogs.

Grizzly bears are left-handed

or,

Usually people suffer the consequences of careless behaviour with stuffed bears more often than with real ones.

A FEW days later I realised I hadn't provided any contact information for anyone who had seen Alex. I made up some little cards with the note, "If you've seen him, please phone . . ." (Obviously I wrote down my phone number, but I'm not giving it out to you. I don't want you to start calling me. I have already said I don't know how to get rid of toadies and hangers-on, so it's better to protect myself from them at the outset).

I walked down the streets where I had posted my signs and attached the cards with my phone number to the ones that were still hanging (some had been stained, covered with other ads, or torn down). It was a lot of work but it gave me something to do. I found 76 ads that were still in a decent condition. That meant that the probability that Alex would be found was 76%. That seemed good enough.

It was the first time I'd ever made signs like those; I didn't have any experience. I had lost things in the past, but had never cared enough to look for them.

Before looking, you should consider whether you really want to find what you've lost. Sometimes it's better to celebrate its disappearance and forget it. I can't think of a single person or object that can't be replaced.

I once read a story in the newspaper about a circus bear. One day, for no reason, he pushed a woman off his cage and ran away. Nobody had expected him to behave that way because the bear was gentle and domesticated. The creature was lost for a long time. The circus owner posted signs all over town, just as I had.

The bear turned up. It came home of its own accord. It just changed its mind and came home. I doubt that it had seen the lost circus bear signs. You'll never believe the first thing it did after coming home! It bit off the owner's hand, the left one, the very one the owner used to pet and feed it. It was impossible to sew the hand back on, although the best doctors in the world tried. After that it got back into its cage and remained as docile as a lamb for the rest of its life.

Nobody could understand what the bear was trying to say, but everyone said over and over again that "it would have been better if the bear hadn't returned." When you search for someone, you expect them to be grateful.

I was searching for the first time and I wondered whether I wouldn't regret it later.

Life: the best of the best
or,
Usually there's no need to live by the principle of necessity.

I KNOW who I was in my previous lives (although I might have mixed up the order of events):

- Blue sludge.
- A flagellum.
- A flagellum again.
- A rock (I spent a good part of my life under water).
- A brachiosaurus (true, I was still in the egg. I never had time to hatch because another dinosaur devoured me; I never saw which one)
- Lightning (I enjoyed that life the most; it was short and bright)
- Australopithecus (I was one of the first to have a reticulated thumb; that's why I could pick things up with my fingers. I died giving birth).
- A Neanderthal (I already knew how to light a fire. I don't know if we burned down the forest out of stupidity or if the fire was caused by lightning. I only know that I died in the fire.)

- The wife of Thor (I didn't like it one bit. You can't imagine how hard it is being a god's wife).
- The hammer of Thor.
- A doctor in India 600 years before Christ (we were the first to profess that health was not fated, that it could be changed through people's efforts. I knew how to produce a large variety of medicines from plants and minerals, I had 125 surgical instruments, I could operate on the nose, the ears, breathing apparatus and cataracts, I knew how to remove stones from internal organs and how to heal broken bones. I could cure physical ailments as well as spiritual ones. I wrote a decent medical guide describing 300 surgical procedures. I classified diseases into eight categories. Despite all that, my name is unknown to history, so I'll write it here. It was Partap Anurada).
- Two-time Olympic gold medalist runner, 4th century BC in Greece (I was killed by other glory-seekers).
- A Buddhist monk in the sixth century (from the moment of my birth I lived in a temple in Huang Yong in Korea. My teacher was the famous Wong Wang. Although in those days nobody counted years, I know that I lived for 102 years. Half of those were spent in nirvana. That's why everyone considered me dead. When I actually died, nobody noticed and so they left me sitting under a tree until I eventually dried up and turned to dust).
- A man of a certain tribe in the seventh century. (It was a very long and cold winter that year and there was famine. While we were hunting, a bear broke my leg.

My bone healed, but one leg remained shorter than the other. I couldn't run fast any longer and I was of no use so my tribe roasted and ate me. It's not a nice fact; that's why I am not naming my tribe).

- An unknown poet (I wrote over 100 poems, but not a single one appealed to anyone and so I never became famous. I grew old and died of shame).
- A knight in eleventh-century Prussia. (I had a lot of land, women and I won several jousting tournaments. After one tournament, drunk, I fell off my horse. I was trampled by the horses of my fellow knights).
- A boy, the son of very poor serfs in Paris. (I died of the Bubonic plague in 1348, barely six months old. I was buried in a mass grave.)
- A slave in Ghana at the end of the 14th-early 15th century. (I worked in the fields. My only wages were sex with my overseers or other slaves several times a day. I can't count how many children I gave birth to. Many died; those who survived were sold as soon as they were old enough to work; I got sick and died young.)
- A troubadour. (I was actually a woman, but to be a woman was difficult and shameful. I don't know what I wanted more, to write or to travel, so I bound my breasts, dressed as a man and began gallivanting through Southern *France* until I grew old, forgot how to write, unbound my breasts and died.)
- The least favourite mistress of a Persian sheikh in the 16th century. (He never loved me; he never came to me at night. He was very wealthy; he had 98 women in his

harem and loved them all more than me. Angry that I was an unsuitable and disobedient lover, the sheikh ordered that I be tied to a stake in the central town square and whipped so that everyone could see what happened to such as I. I baked in the sun. In a few months I would have turned thirteen.)

- A nightingale. (I admit, in a cage. It was the 17th century and the Emperor Kangxi was only seven years old when he inherited the throne. On that occasion, I was given him as a gift. During his sixty-one-year reign, I hung in his bedroom. We conferred on how to unify China, how to win obedience from Taiwan, Mongolia, Korea and how to stop the Russians. I also helped him write the introduction to the famous Kangxi dictionary. He always asked for my advice and I always responded. The Emperor understood my language perfectly. The second he died, I turned into a plume of smoke and dispersed through the bars of the cage.)

- A shaman in Buriatia. (I knew how to locate a patient's lost soul and reunite it with its body. I got along well with the gods which was why they helped us during famine or drought. I could travel to heaven or to the depths of the earth and return again. My drums were my carriage, carrying me to other worlds. I served my people and they loved and feared me. The one time I was careless and got too close to the evil spirits, they possessed me and I couldn't return to the earthly world. This pleased my disciple.)

- A pig. (No typo; I was an ordinary, simple pig. You can easily guess my fate.)

- Louis Pasteur. (Yes, it was I, who in the 19th century discovered microorganisms and learned that they can be destroyed at high temperatures).
- Starbuck. (Led by Captain Ahab, Stubb, Queequeg, Tashtego, Daggoo, the other sailors and I set out to sea in the mighty Pequod to catch the Great White Whale. As you know, he destroyed our boat and we all drowned in the blue ocean depths. But I can't complain; it was an interesting hunt and a great voyage.)
- The son of a woman from Earth and a male creature from another planet. (This life was utter nonsense. I lived on Earth, but was a stranger to everyone. I lived several hundred earthly years because time is calculated differently on my father's planet; they live much longer there, and we all, as you know, inherit some things from our mothers, and some things from our fathers. I encountered all kinds of problems associated with these types of situations. I could not have any close friends; I was always moving from one place to another, so that nobody would guess what I was; I was afraid of telling the truth about myself. I was afraid to admit it to myself. (I can't say from whom I inherited this feature). I would pretend that I had a strange disease and I even believed it myself for a while. During my long life I acquired a good education, amassed a great amount of wealth, loved countless women and men, made a lot of children, but they all died before I did. Finally I grew old. I died happy and alone in an abandoned castle in Montenegro. I left my wealth to a poor, young, lonely neighbour. Neither she nor I understood why.)

- In my most recent past life, I was a female prison guard. I worked with extremely hardened and dangerous criminals. (And, yes, I was cruel. I kicked and beat them – not as much as they needed, but as much as I wanted. Nobody controlled the guards, and prisons in those days were prisons, not spas. If one of the prisoners dared to make a peep or to resist my orders, I beat her to death. I didn't know how else to behave with them. After all they were murderers; some had killed their own children. I won't pretend that I tried to punish or rehabilitate them. I simply enjoyed the feeling of power. I enjoyed beating them until they were pieces of meat, kicking them until they stopped yelling and then, gurgling. I remember one especially well. She asked me to pity her. Her victim had probably begged the same of her, but I doubt she heeded her. Why should I pity her? I beat her with all my heart. There is nothing to be done about it. That's what I was like: calm, cold blooded, and unconquerable. I died young because those conspiring bitches stabbed me. They lured me into the cellar and cut my throat. All I remember is them watching my agony and laughing.)

I am living, now, my twenty-eighth life and I am emptiness, although I often pretend I am a person.

In my next life I will be an electric eel. (I don't want to be, but it's not my choice).

Gold

or,

Usually you can have whatever you want. But you don't want.

GOLD IS the most reprocessed material in the world: 85% of the gold that has been discovered is still in use.

ONE MORNING, Illinois said in all seriousness that he was fed up and that he was going drop everything and go to Alaska to pan for gold. I didn't understand why he needed to pan for gold; the stores were, after all, full of it. But Illinois wasn't joking.

Red Dress cried and begged him not to go. I didn't cry, but I was sad too. I thought that perhaps I should go with him. I would find gold; I would make myself rings and earrings. (It would be hard to convince myself that I needed them, but I would try).

"Leave, all of you. Go to the moon if you like." Greek pretended that he was indifferent, but I could see that he too was sad.

When I told Illinois that I was going with him, he was happy and began to pack his things. I would have packed as well but I didn't know what to pack. Would you know what to pack for a trip to Alaska to pan for gold?

By evening the idea no longer seemed such a great one. I didn't know why, but I no longer wanted to go.

"Listen, Illinois, why don't we try to find gold here instead?" I suggested and he agreed heartily.

"If you're with me, then I'm happy here too."

Such trite expressions irritated me, but I wanted Illinois to stay, so I didn't say anything. Besides, he knew how to say it easily, without any commitment.

We agreed to meet that evening after work. I asked Greek to allow me leave work early. Greek wanted to know if I was leaving work early because I was leaving for good. Could he expect me the next day at work? I said that I never planned my life several days into the future.

I dressed for the evening in a light azure dress, the most beautiful one that I had. I would never let Illinois cut it, even if he begged me.

We had agreed to meet at the fountain. I arrived first. I waited and waited, but Illinois didn't arrive. I thought that perhaps I had mixed up the time or place as I often did. I waited a little longer, then decided to walk around the fountain ten times. If Illinois didn't come, I decided I would go home. I walked slowly, but he didn't come. Ten more times, I decided, but I wouldn't wait any longer. I traversed the fountain ten more times, and still he did not arrive. I sat on the edge of the fountain and closed my eyes. At that moment Illinois sat down beside me.

"I got here first, but I waited on the other side of the street. I wanted to watch you arrive, to see how you would wait. I wanted to convince myself that you're as beautiful as I thought."

"I walked laps around the fountain." I said the first thing that popped into my head to interrupt him, because I was afraid he would say, "I got a good look at you and you're ugly."

People often said that to me.

"Didn't you get dizzy?"

"I was dizzy before I got here," I said.

If it were not for Alex, I could have fallen in love with Illinois. But I couldn't.

Illinois was dressed in black as always. Black was so attractive on him that I couldn't think of anything else – only that I wanted to touch him.

"I forgot to kiss you. May I now?"

I really don't like it when people frame the question like that. It's easy enough to answer a simple, "No, you can't." Then you say it and that's that. But how do you tell them they may? Do you say, "Please, of course, whenever you want"? Or simply, "Yes, please"?

Illinois, tired of waiting for an answer, simply leaned over and kissed me. It was better than the first time. His lips were dry and wrinkled. He was frightened, as if he were kissing me for the first time. He did everything as if it were the first (or last) time. Everything seemed important; everything was frightening and attractive. He loved me painfully and seductively.

"Listen, my little deer, have you forgotten that we came here to search for gold?"

"I don't think there's any reason to shove off to Alaska just for that."

"So you believe you can find what you're looking for without leaving home, that all you have to do is look?" Illinois wanted to know.

"Quite," I agreed.

That evening, Illinois actually found a gold ring, just like that, in the street. As he was walking he almost stepped on it. The ring was scratched and ugly and too large for me, but I couldn't argue: it was gold.

"You planted it here." I couldn't believe it.

"Yes, and I arranged with all the passers-by not to pick it up," Iliinois said.

I wore the ring from that day on, along with Alex's mother's ruby octopus ring. I had to wear both rings on one finger because Illinois's ring was too big and it would have fallen off otherwise.

"What shall we do now?"

"I don't know. I don't have anything planned." Illinois laughed. "We went out to search for gold; I thought it would take longer."

Have nothing to do we kissed, which is, I think, a great way to spend time. Better than fishing, for example.

I asked him at what moment with me he had been happiest. He said it was the same moment that I'd felt happiest with him. Try asking your lover this question; I guarantee your answers will not correspond.

Remembering then my old game, stone-faced, I turned to Illinois.

"Excuse me. Do I know you?" I said.

"No,"

For a moment I was confused, not expecting such a response. I hadn't played in a long time; my skills were rusty.

"Don't even try to touch me. I don't allow strangers to touch me."

"Fine."

Illinois was completely at ease, not in the least bit surprised. I turned and started to walk away in the opposite direction. Illinois paid no attention. He continued where he was headed.

I walked a long distance until I could no longer see him, then I grew frightened and made my way back. Illinois was waiting for me. When I rejoined him, he was silent.

"I don't know you," I repeated.

"You don't even know my name."

"So what?"

"If you behave, I'll tell you." He laughed.

He grabbed me by my waist, lifted me up, and placed me on the ledge of the fountain. I stood there like a memorial to victims of war. I didn't know what to say or do. Illinois held me close. I let his hair down. His hair was very beautiful. One day he had told us that he was thinking of cutting it, but Red Dress cried and begged him not to, and Illinois relented.

We spent half the night walking. The whole time I wanted to touch him, but I didn't dare.

"Do you know what Red Dress's name is?" I asked.

"Of course. Everyone does."

"I didn't know," I said and it sounded rather sad.

"It's not such a big deal," Illinois laughed. "You haven't missed anything."

If it were not for Alex I really could have fallen in love with Illinois. But unfortunately, I couldn't.

But I miss his sad freedom, his longing and his unrequited love.

Everything is an illusion; illusions
are the foundation of the world

or,

Usually things move quicker as
you approach the ending.

THIS ISN'T really the end of the story. Everything was
just beginning, so have patience and you'll find out what
happened next.

That summer there were wild storms and a heat wave. A
lightning bolt set fire to the building next door. By the time
the firefighters arrived, the building had burned down to its
foundations. Nothing happened to *France*; it wasn't even
smoke damaged, though we were all frightened. If something
burns down once, it won't burn again. Fire is like chicken pox,
you get it once and develop an immunity to it. Greek should
have been grateful to me; I made *France* secure for all time.

(*France* really did stay open for another one hundred
years. After Greek's death, his son, who nobody had ever
heard of, took over. Greek had seven wives and seven children, but in his will, he left *France* only to his son. I don't
know how he chose which child he would leave everything
to; I imagine he played rock, paper, scissors.

The heir showed up after Greek's funeral. He introduced
himself and announced that he was the new owner. I don't

know if the workers liked him; I hadn't been working at *France* for a long time. As far as I heard, the new owner was cheerful; he managed to drink up *France's* profits in a half a year. A Chinese family bought the premises and opened an Asian restaurant. The place changed hands often after that; a fast food restaurant first, then a pancake house; later a fancy molecular food restaurant, a wine bar, a kebab house, a kosher restaurant, a confectionary, a halal restaurant and a chocolate shop.

Not a single owner changed the name. *France* remained *France*. I think that was fitting. Why change the name, even if it wasn't really appropriate? Would you, for example, want to constantly change your name? Your life changes, your environment changes, your landlords, but your name remains.)

Without even noticing how, I ended up being with Illinois constantly. It just happened. Life was so light and easy with him that I stayed. I don't know if he was determined to be happy or if it happened by accident, but he was always happy. Ants never sleep and Illinois never cried; he never looked for someone to blame; he never asked to be loved and, without any pangs of conscience, he did whatever shot into his head. It was pleasant and easy to be with him.

We would walk holding hands. We would feed his birds. Dance. Illinois was never alone. As soon as we parted, he would be off to meet someone else. He was just the kind of person everyone needed and one who was often used. I don't think there was anything wrong with this. Everyone needs and so everyone takes.

* * *

One morning, Greek's soul had reason to celebrate.

Walking in through the door to *France* he announced to everyone that Not-Alex had moved in with Polina. Greek seemed happy (he even bought a goldfish and dropped it into the old goldfish bowl). It explained why Anastasia had been drinking coffee alone for the past week. What could you do? You can't have everything.

Anastasia blamed me for everything, I don't know why. I didn't argue. After all, she was a lawyer; she understood these things better than I.

Red Dress changed as well. She started to dress in white. I wouldn't say that she looked like a swan, but she looked lovely.

Alex was still missing, but I sensed he was coming. Nobody arrived unannounced and if you paid attention, you would notice the warning signs.

I'm here

or,

Usually the greatest joy is in surrender, in being trampled and crushed under foot.

THAT MORNING I woke at six. I never get up that early, but that day I did. I knew something was going to happen.

I showered and put on some makeup. If something was going to happen, I needed to be ready. I dressed comfortably; I don't know why. Just in case.

I didn't let the box out of my hands. I had to find Alex and return it to him.

But I didn't have to search. At eight o'clock Alex arrived. Barely in the door, he asked if it was eight. I checked his watch and said that it was three minutes past. Alex said that he was glad. Everything that had a beginning had to have an ending. I had no idea what he was talking about.

"Will you have some coffee?" I asked.

"No."

"As you like," I said. He would realise that with me he could do whatever he liked.

"Listen," Alex said.

Why did he say that? I always listened to him.

"Listen," he repeated. "I'm leaving."

So what? So what if he was leaving? Even if it was for a long time, I could wait.

"Don't call me or write," Alex said.

How funny, I thought. I never called him or wrote.

"It's over," he said abruptly.

So what if it was over? We could start all over again, I thought. I would try really hard to start all over again.

"Don't forget your box," I said.

Alex turned and looked me in the eyes for the first time. I liked that. It was a good sign. If he looked me in the eyes, it meant that he loved me.

But Alex began to shout.

"Do you understand that I have no use for that box?" (No, I didn't. Besides, the box wasn't mine). "Neither you nor the box." (This I understood even less. Why did he feel the need to repeat the same thing over and over. I wasn't deaf). "Leave me alone!" (He probably didn't realise that if he were with me, he would be alone. Maybe I should have told him? But I didn't say anything).

"Will you have some coffee?" I asked again. I thought that a cup of coffee would calm his nerves and we could discuss how we could start all over again.

But Alex didn't want coffee. He stepped over to me, turned me around gently and slowly pushed me forward. I liked that. We were by the armoire. Alex opened the armoire door with one hand, while with the other he held me fast. (He couldn't let me go, I thought). Then he let go. He pressed both my arms around my back and gently pushed me again. Having nowhere else to move, I got into the armoire. There was plenty of room. Alex waited until I got inside then closed the door and locked it. I heard the key turn in the lock. After that Alex turned on the radio, loud enough so that I could hear it and left.

I liked that he cared about me. He was going out, so he put me somewhere safe so that I wouldn't get lost before he returned. I dreamed of what would happen when he returned.

But he didn't return. I sat and waited for him for a long time. It began to get dark. The doors were not airtight and the darkness entered the armoire through the cracks. That's when I died. I had no more reason to live and so I died.

It got completely dark; I could no longer see anything. It was best to wait for morning. I checked all my pockets. I found a hundred things, but most importantly, a nail file. In the morning, by daylight, I would unscrew the lock and climb out.

I lay down and curled up into a ball. People don't love us when we most need it, I thought. But it was not a big deal. I would wait. I would sit there and wait.

I imagined that the sky was above me. I saw the stars twinkling. There was even a shooting star and I made a wish (I wished for a present. There are two types of women: those who give gifts and those who receive them. I was the first type, but I wanted this to change).

After that I imagined I was dancing. All alone. The music that Alex had left on for me wasn't really suitable for dancing to, but I couldn't imagine anything else while the song played.

I don't know when I fell asleep. I wasn't scared or sad. Maybe because I was dead. In the eternal silence.

When I awoke, it was still dark. Although there was plenty of room to stretch out in the armoire, my body was numb. I tried to move. The music was still playing. Only then did I notice that I had the box with me in the armoire. I was pleased that it hadn't got lost. I could return it to Alex.

I had no idea what time it was. I hoped that Alex would come back and ask, "Is it eight?" I waited, but he didn't come.

The darkness was what bothered me most. I couldn't see anything, so I had to wait until it got light outside. My entire body ached. I couldn't find a position that would allow me to rest. It was hot and I was thirsty. Some moments, everything around me vanished and only a grey stickiness remained, like a thick, dirty, fog. Then it would become cold and sad, but these feelings would quickly pass. I would lay still and dream.

I fell asleep and dreamt of Alex.

Afterwards, but not as a result of
or,
Usually your way of thinking changes according to your situation.

WORKING AS a schoolteacher, Dalton wrote an English language grammar. "It must be accepted as an axiom that time in the real sense of the term can exist only in the past or future tenses. Nonetheless, for the purposes of language, we also have to admit the existence of a present tense, which expresses a short moment of being. It encompasses the past and the future. Phrases like 'now' and 'at this moment' comprise the limits separating these tenses."

WHAT IS now simply doesn't exist. I have always known this. Everything either was or will be. What is now truly is not.

I worked for a long time until I finally managed to unscrew the armoire's lock. The screws were old and stuck with an invisible paste, which made it hard for them to budge. I thought about moving out of the house. It was too much like me.

After dismantling the lock, I kicked repeatedly until the doors opened.

Why did those bloody doors creak so much?

It's not worth it
or,
Usually square things can roll although by their design they shouldn't.

OUR STUDIES aren't for nothing. Everything we learn eventually comes in handy. Even if it's only how to kick.

The first person I ran into when I got outside was Anastasia.

I didn't know if she was aiming at me or at herself, but she ended up kicking the box.

The same wounded bird flew over Anastasia.

The box split in two; the lid rolled over to the other side of the street.

It's not worth trying to keep things safe. They're eternal, never ending.

It's not worth to keep hold of people. They're eternal, never ending.

I'm so sorry
or,
Usually boxes contain precisely
what you weren't expecting.

I'M SO sorry. The box contained inert gases.

OBVIOUSLY, FOR the citations I used Wikipedia..

Visit us at

www.noirpress.co.uk

Follow us
@PressNoir